The Camp Follower Affair

Mary Fraser in the Ohio Country

ROBERT J SHADE

Sunshine Hill Press

First Edition 2015
Sunshine Hill Press, LLC
2937 Novum Road
Reva, VA 22735

Artwork with specific permission:
Front Cover: *The Camp Followers* by Pamela Patrick White
(www.whitehistoricart.com)

The Camp Follower Affair is a work of fiction. With the exception of historical people, places, and certain events in the narrative, all names, characters, places, and incidents are used fictitiously. Any resemblance to current events, places, or living persons is entirely coincidental.

ISBN-10: 0692408541
ISBN-13: 9780692408544

MAJOR CHARACTERS

Historical

Henry Bouquet	Colonel, 60th Foot, Commander of British Forces Pennsylvania
Thomas Stirling	Captain, 42nd Foot (Black Watch)
Asher Clayton	Lieutenant Colonel, 2nd Battalion, Pennsylvania Regiment
Thomas Hutchins	Ensign, 60th Foot, Engineer of British Ohio Expedition
Robert Kirkwood	Corporal, 42nd Foot (Black Watch), formerly of 77th Foot
Charlot Kaske	Shawnee war captain
Simon Girty	Captive of Mingo tribe

Fictional

Mary Fraser	Camp follower and nurse in 42nd Foot (Black Watch)
Joshua Baird	Civilian scout for Colonel Bouquet
Richard Grenough	Owner of border trading company
Reginald Welford	Lieutenant, 60th Foot, Colonel Bouquet's adjutant
Percy Munro	Surgeon of 42nd Foot (Black Watch)
Charles Highsmith	Contract surgeon of Pennsylvania Regiment
Abigail Gibson	Captive of Mingo Indians, known as Orenda
Charles McDonald	Captain, 42nd Foot (Black Watch)

Timothy McGregor	Private in Captain Stirling's Company of the 42nd Foot
Ian Tavish	McDonald's bagpiper
Kathryn O'Hara	Nurse in 42nd Foot (Black Watch)
Wolf Claw	War captain of Slippery Rock Creek Mingo

CONTENTS

CHAPTER ONE
Gathering at Fort Pitt

The wagon landed on its side with a resounding crash which echoed through the forest. Mary Fraser stood in the mud at the edge of the wagon track, looking down from the hillock at the great blue Conestoga as it lay on its left side in the gully, the two right-side wheels still slowly revolving in the air. Three of the bows which supported the canvas cover had snapped, tearing the cover wide open. Several trunks had spilled out through the hole in the cover as the wagon tipped onto its side and now lay alongside the wagon bed. One of them had broken open and scattered medical instruments around the ground. Surgeon Munro, Orderly Taggart, and the other nurses of the Black Watch stood with Mary, all of them silently staring down at the wreck.

Kathryn O'Hara shook her head and said with her usual understatement, "Sure 'n that's a proper mess, Mr. Munro."

Munro looked over at the contract waggoner, who was working to calm his team of six horses. When the wagon had rolled off of the trail, it had snapped the pin which connected the front axle assembly to the tongue, so the team had not been dragged down by the weight of the wagon and now stood, agitated but unharmed, up on the wagon track. The surgeon said quietly, but with great irony in his voice, "McLane, it would have been much better if you had managed to stay on the road."

"I tell you, it weren't my fault," exclaimed the driver. "It's all this rain we been have'n. The side of the road turned to mud and gave way under them left wheels."

"The other wagons seem to have made it through here safely." Munro looked over at the driver with a grim look on his face.

"That was earlier in the day, sir. Way earlier. It weren't so wet back then. You know it's been raining on and off all day." Then he said accusingly, "If we hadn't started so late, we'd a' made it through like the others."

Munro sighed. "McLane, you know all that was unavoidable. We had that emergency surgery at last night's campsite. So we couldn't leave with the rest of the convoy."

The wagoner exclaimed, "I'll tell you what I *do* know. We ain't gonna get that wagon back on the road with just this team. We're gonna' have to lighten it so we can push it back up on its wheels and we'll need to have at least another team hooked up to pull it out." He looked around, rather unnecessarily, and said, "An' I don't see nary another team 'round here."

Mary could remain silent no longer. "Maybe if McLane hadn't been taking long nips all day from that jug he keeps in the side-box on the wagon, he'd have been able to see the soft mud at the side of the road."

McLane scowled. "Keep that sharp tongue of yours still, you little red-haired tart. This ain't none of your concern."

Munro snapped back at the waggoner, "I'll have you keep a civil tongue in your mouth toward my nurses, McLane."

Mary pointed up at the sun, half hidden by a cloud and now low on the western sky. "It will be our great concern if we have to camp out here all night waiting for help to come back from the column. And we don't have anything to eat."

Surgeon Munro nodded. "Miss Fraser is quite right. We need to get help as fast as possible." He turned to the orderly. "Taggart, you'll have to take my horse and ride up to the convoy. They're undoubtedly encamped at Bushy Run Station by now. It's only about three or four miles ahead. Go straight to the convoy commander, Captain McDonald. Tell him about our problem and that we need at least one more Conestoga team. And he must send a full squad of soldiers with strong backs." He waved to the four nurses. "These women can't get that wagon upright."

Taggart sighed. "Aye, sir." Then, not being an experienced rider, he mounted the surgeon's horse rather tentatively and soon disappeared to the westward along Forbes Road.

Munro started down the slope to where the wagon lay. "Ladies, I said I'd not expect you to help right the wagon. But there's certainly no reason you can't assist with unloading it. Shall we get started?"

They had been at work for perhaps half an hour when Kathryn suddenly stood still, then put her hand to ear and said, "I hear noise of horses and wagons in the distance."

Munroe stood up from repacking the spilled chest and said, "That seems rather too soon to be from the convoy."

Mary heard the sounds also, but said nothing. Instead she laboriously climbed the bank up to the road, slipping and sliding in the mud. She looked westward, but saw no sign of anyone approaching from the direction of Bushy Run. McLane, who had not deigned to assist with the unloading, had been lounging on a fallen log, his jug — which had miraculously survived the wreck — beside him. He burped, then pointed in the other direction. "There be horsemen and wagons a'commin' from the east. I caught sight of them crossing a ridge a little while ago."

Mary snapped, "I guess it was too much trouble to mention it to us." Then she looked in that direction and immediately caught sight of a rider visible at the top of a low ridge, sitting his horse and taking in the scene of the accident. Then another rider appeared and stopped beside the first. The two men carried out a short discussion, then spurred their mounts forward.

Mary called down to inform Munro and then took a few steps toward the approaching horsemen. The man she had first seen was well dressed. He wore a dark brown coat, tan breeches, with highly polished leather riding boots which reached nearly to the knee. On his head was a fine beaver hat with a round crown. A brace of horse pistols were holstered in front of his saddle and he carried a short riding crop in his right hand. The second man was obviously a retainer, dressed in rough working clothes including a short shell jacket, breeches with cloth leggings, and a hat with turned up brim. As she watched, three Conestogas came into view. In addition to the drivers there were seven or eight men walking alongside the wagons.

The well-dressed man pulled up his horse in front of Mary. He touched his hat to her, motioned toward the overturned wagon, and said, "It appears that you're having a spot of trouble."

Mary replied, "Mister, we could handle a spot of trouble with no problem. But this is more like a *lake* of trouble. And we're sunk into the middle of it!"

The man grinned. "Well, young lady, it would be our pleasure to help extract you from the lake." He turned to the man beside him and said, "McCrae, lead all the wagons up beyond this wreck, then bring one of the teams back to help get that wagon out of the gulley. And get the rest of the men organized to right that wagon."

By now Munro, puffing from the effort to climb the hill, had arrived. "Good day, sir. I'm Surgeon Munro of the 42nd. I'd be much obliged If you could see your way clear to assist us."

"Naturally, sir. I've already told the young lady here it would be our pleasure. I have several teams and a dozen strong backs available, Mr. Munro. And it is *always* my honor to assist His Majesty's forces."

Robert J Shade

The man, who Mary guessed was in his mid-forties but very well preserved, with only a hint of thickening at the waist, doffed his hat and made a small bow to Munro. "Permit me to introduce myself. I am Richard Grenough, of York, sir. A merchant providing supplies to Colonel Bouquet's expedition."

Munro smiled broadly. "Grenough! Why certainly I have heard of you. But you are too modest, sir! I read how you advised the colonial government during the recent Paxton Boy Insurrection. And if the Pennsylvania Gazette is to be believed, you were of great assistance to Doctor Franklin in negotiating the accord with those Ulster-Scot rogues which ended the uprising."

"I plead guilty to offering a few ideas to the good doctor and sharing my knowledge of the western border people with him. But I would be remiss if I took any credit for the work done by the brilliant Doctor Franklin, sir."

Munro nodded and continued. "And now I understand that you are to act as one of the commissioners for treating with the Indians once we bring the savages to negotiations."

Grenough swung down from the saddle and offered his hand to the surgeon. "Once again, you are correct, Mr. Munro. Colonel Bouquet and I have worked together on many occasions and I'm indeed proud to call him my personal friend." He motioned in a generally westward direction and said, "I'm looking forward to arriving at Fort Pitt and meeting with Henry."

The three of them moved aside as Grenough's wagons carefully transited the muddy hill. The first wagon was driven expertly by a burley, broad shouldered waggoner. Mary noticed that he limped on his left side. But then she was shocked when the man looked at her as the wagon passed. His face was terribly misshapen, particularly on the left side. His cheekbone was mashed in, the ridge bone of his left eye appeared to have been crushed, his nose smashed nearly flat, and it was clear that he had lost his front teeth. There were scars all over his face. Mary instinctively put her hand to her mouth at the sight and averted her eyes in embarrassment.

When the wagon had passed, Grenough, who had seen her reaction, leaned over and said softly, "Mr. Bratton is my lead waggoner and a very good man. But unfortunately he lost his looks in a vicious tavern fight over a faithless tart. And I'm sad to say his brains were disturbed and he's never again been quite right in the head." He paused for a moment and an angry look came over his face; then he continued, "The man who beat him is a vicious, conniving German who is known to have killed in cold blood."

Mary looked up at the merchant. "That's interesting, Mr. Grenough. I once knew a young German; he was a fine lad; kind, gentle, and loving."

4

Grenough smiled and said gently, "Naturally, Miss, I didn't mean to imply that all Germans were vicious."

Once the wagons had all passed, several of Grenough's men descended the hill and without much trouble heaved the wagon to an upright position.

Meanwhile McCrae, a burly, black-haired Irishman, had surveyed the muddy road. He looked down scornfully at McLane, who was still on the log with the jug in his hands and clearly in his cups. Then he turned to Grenough and said, "By the Saints, any bloody fool could have gotten that wagon over this patch if he'd been paying attention."

Grenough walked over to McLane and scowled at him.

McLane looked up and shook his head. "See here, Cap'n, that ain't fair. That Irishman weren't here when it happened. I was doing my best; just misjudged how solid the ground was, that's all."

Grenough had been tapping his riding crop against his right boot; suddenly he raised the crop and then with a swift, powerful motion struck the jug out of McLane's hands. It flew against a tree and smashed. Then he turned and said to McCrae, "Have one of our men drive this man's rig into the camp at Bushy Run to make sure it gets there safely." Then he looked at Munro. "Surgeon, I submit that you should permanently replace this scoundrel as soon as possible. I expect you could arrange that at Fort Pitt. Meanwhile, I believe if you explain the situation to Captain McDonald he'll arrange for an appropriate punishment for this driver." He looked down at McLane. "Most likely something which would take place while he was lashed barebacked to a wagon wheel."

McLane was not too drunk to miss Grenough's meaning. A look of horror came over his face.

By this time all of the nurses had joined the group on the road. Bratton, the man with the disfigured face, was leading a team from one of Grenough's wagons back to help pull the surgical wagon out of the gulley. Another man had re-hitched McLane's team to the now upright Conestoga. Grenough turned to Munro. "We'll hitch my team ahead of your team, and together they should have enough strength to get the wagon back up to the road."

Munro made profuse thanks to Grenough.

Grenough shook his head. "Not at all, Mr. Munro; it's my pleasure to help." He motioned to all the nurses and bowed slightly. Then he looked directly into Mary's eyes, hesitated a moment, a smile on his face.

Mary looked into the man's eyes and felt a disturbing sense of excitement.

Then Grenough continued, still looking at Mary, "I could not have lived with myself if I had left these lovely ladies marooned in the bush away from the comforts of an established camp."

With that, he turned and walked over to where he could personally supervise the efforts of the waggoners.

Kathryn nudged Mary in the arm. "Now ain't he the nicest gentleman?"

Mary nodded. "Indeed he is; he certainly knows how to get things organized." She looked at Grenough directing the salvage of the wagon, and felt a surge of admiration at the man's confidence and obvious competence. She turned back to Kathryn. "We're lucky to have such a man helping Colonel Bouquet on this expedition."

* * *

"Smartly now, men, let's get these tents up. And corporal, I'll caution you to take care we get them in proper straight rows. Remember, we'll need a wide space between the two rows so we can maneuver litters easily. We're right under the parapet here and I don't want Colonel Reid of the 42nd or even Colonel Bouquet giving me grief about the hospital lacking in military standards." Munro was directing a sharp faced, red-haired corporal with a thick chest and broad shoulders who was leading a detail of the Black Watch which had been assigned to help set up the hospital.

The corporal faced Munro, stood to attention, and gave the surgeon a crooked smile. He said, "Now do 'na worry a wee bit, sir; we'll get you set up proper-like in no time. The hospital will look as regimental as any company in the battalion."

The surgeon nodded. "See you do that, Corporal. And then help these nurses unload the wagon and stow the medical supplies and equipment in the proper tents. Taggart and Miss Fraser will tell you where to put things." He paused and looked over at Mary Fraser. "I'll be going over to meet with the adjutant, Miss Fraser. I should be back in a couple of hours." Having admonished the corporal, Munro adjusted his bonnet and strode off toward the main gate of Fort Pitt.

Mary and Kathryn had stood by watching the proceedings, barely able to keep straight faces.

As soon as the surgeon was out of earshot, the corporal turned to Mary and broke into a wide grin. "Mary, my beautiful lass, I was up on the parapet when Captain McDonald's column arrived. And my eyeballs nearly jumped out of my

Taggart had brought out his fiddle. It was his proudest possession and he had real talent in playing the instrument; it seemed to come alive in his hands. Mary could see the great pleasure in his face as he prepared to play. Soon his bright tunes were enhancing the joyous atmosphere. After a few sprightly tunes, the group began to sing songs of home interspersed with jovial tavern songs. Presently Taggart stopped to rest, and Tavish took over, standing beside the fire, playing the pipes. The sound brought people from nearby fires and soon the crowd had grown to large proportions.

Kirkwood, grinning broadly, walked out in front of the fire, a broadsword in each hand. He exclaimed to the company, "Now, me lads and lassies, we'll be see'in who can hold their spirits!" He laid the swords on the ground in the shape of an 'X' and shouted, "Who'll be the first?"

Mary laughed and called out, "It's you who put the swords down, Bob! You damn well should be the first!"

There was a universal cry of agreement from all the men and women around the fire. Kirkwood looked perplexed for a moment, then raised his hands and shrugged his shoulders in signal of surrender. He waved to Tavish and called, "Do your worst, Ian!" He stepped over to the swords, and waited for the piping to begin.

Tavish responded with one of his fastest tunes. Kirkwood laughed and then started his dance, his feet moving rapidly in the spaces between the swords, his hands high in the air. Mary was impressed to see that — despite the copious amount of drink he had consumed — Kirkwood was able to maintain the precise control of himself which was required to keep from landing on either of the sword blades. When Tavish finished his tune, Kirkwood jumped away from the swords to the clapping of the crowd. He acknowledged the applause with a broad grin and the wave of his hand.

Kirkwood came and sat down beside Mary. She squeezed his arm and whispered, "You're as good as you ever were, Bob."

"Do 'na you ever doubt it, Mary!" Then he winked at her, and a mischievous smile came over his face. He shouted out, "Let's have young Tim McGregor!"

A wave of laughter rolled through the assemblage. Then the men from the 42nd started shouting: McGregor! McGregor! We want McGregor!"

Kirkwood leaned over and said to Mary, "McGregor's the youngest man in Stirling's company. He's not yet twenty."

"How can there be someone so young? The 42nd has been here in the colonies for more than seven years."

Kirkwood waved his finger. "When we was reorganized last year, there wasn't enough of the old crowd left over to bring the battalion up to full strength."

Mary looked puzzled: "Even with the men from the 77th who decided to transfer?"

"No, they needed new men, even to meet just the peacetime establishment. So they shipped over a draft from the barracks in Scotland, Mary. McGregor was one of them." He smiled. "He's so young, the lad's become the pet of the company."

As they spoke, a young highlander was propelled to his feet by comrades and pushed toward the crossed swords.

Mary saw that he was wobbly on his feet, but had put on a game face. "He's feeling his drink," she said to Kirkwood.

"All the better for our amusement," Kirkwood said with a roguish grin. "Anyway, we've all had our embarrassing moments dancing over the swords. Sure and I've provided merriment for watchers often enough. Ask anyone from the 77th."

Mary looked at the young man closely. He was of a tall and wiry build, with light colored hair. He had blue eyes and a pleasant face, which at the moment had taken on a determined look as he attempted to shake off the effects of the alcohol and get control of his limbs.

The music began and the youth started his dance. Mary found herself impressed with the almost feminine grace of his moves as he stepped delicately into the spaces between the swords. He danced with one hand on his hip, the other in the air, periodically holding both hands upward and then changing back to his hand-on-hip stance.

Mary noticed that as he danced, the expression on McGregor's face became more confident and his movements bolder. Finally his face broke into an outright grin and it was clear he was enjoying himself. She turned to Kirkwood. "It looks like your friend is not a stranger to the dance."

Kirkwood shrugged. "Indeed, lass, he's 'na doing too bad. An' as I always say, a man who can drink and then dance makes a fine mate for the company."

Mary turned back to watch, and at that moment McGregor got into trouble. Tavish was finishing his tune and McGregor was preparing to jump away from the swords. But in so doing, he placed one foot awkwardly and then tripped and stumbled toward the fire. He instinctively reached out with his hands to catch himself, and when he did fall, his left hand landed in the edge of the fire.

There was a collective shout from all the watchers. McGregor's mouth opened in a silent scream as his hand was burned by the coals. He quickly pushed himself out of the fire and rolled onto his back, clutching his left hand with the right. Mary knew that the pain must be excruciating, but the highlander gritted his teeth in shock and made no sound as he stared down at his burned hand.

Suddenly Surgeon Munro was there, having pushed his way through the crowd. Mary realized he must have been watching from the edge of the gathering. He bent over McGregor, examining his left hand. The surgeon looked up and surveyed the crowd. He called for Taggart and then to Kathryn and motioned for both of them to join him. Then the three of them helped McGregor to his feet. Mary jumped up and joined the group by the fire.

"Can I help?" She asked.

Munro, still examining McGregor's hand, looked up at her and shook his head. "No, I'll not need you, Mary. Kathryn will be enough help. You stay here and enjoy yourself."

Mary stood by the fire watching as they helped the youth toward the hospital tents. Then the crowd, which had been watching silently, started with another shout. "Mary! Mary! Mary dance!"

Kirkwood called out from his seat, "They'll not be satisfied till they see you dance to the pipes, lass!"

"You put them up to this, didn't you, Bob?" She stood looking down at the corporal as the calls for her to dance grew louder and began to be accompanied by clapping.

"Now lass, everyone knows how much you love dancing. And all the young lads have been waiting, 'cause they love watching you as much as you like dancing. You're 'na going to let them down are you?"

Now the calls were increasing, coming from all around the fire circle. Mary smiled. The truth was she did love to dance; to lose herself in the music and to allow her spirit soar away from the drudgery of life. So Mary permitted herself to be convinced. She was still in her improvised marching outfit, which she had put together from cast-off uniform parts. For comfort, she unbuttoned the red waist-length jacket, allowing her white uniform shirt to show, and hitched up the long ankle-length skirt which she had pieced together from two soldier's kilts. Men cheered and whistled as the lower part of her legs came into view. She grinned back at them and then snugged the blue bonnet down on her hair to ensure it wouldn't fly off as she jumped and twirled.

Then she waved to Tavish to start the pipes. He nodded, but then smiled and motioned to Taggart. The two of them conferred for a moment and then both of them began a duet, pipes and fiddle playing the same tune. The people around the fire clapped enthusiastically.

Mary tapped her foot for a moment in concert with the tune, and then started her dance. It was one of her best times above the swords. She had had enough drink from Kirkwood's jug to feel playful, but not enough to impair her movements and balance. She had the sense of being as light as a bird and agile as a squirrel running and leaping through the branches of a tree. Her feet seemed to hardly touch the ground. She was spurred on by the appreciative shouts and clapping of the soldiers.

It seemed as if Tavish and his partner played for a long time, repeating the tune over and over. Mary lost track of how long she danced. But finally, the music stopped and she jumped to a stop in front of the swords, her arms above her head and a broad smile on her face. There was a long and resounding cheer from all around the fire, men and women alike.

After a few seconds, Mary put her hands down. Kirkwood stood up and held out the jug to her. Seeing it, she suddenly felt incredibly thirsty. Walking to him, she reached for the jug and, putting her head back, took a long gulp of the liquid. The whiskey burned as it went down, but immediately gave her a warm feeling which enhanced the glow she was already feeling. Mary lowered the jug and looked into the faces of a score of smiling soldiers, who now cheered her prowess at the jug as enthusiastically as they had her dancing.

Then, just behind the crowd, she saw two men standing and watching her. One was dressed in the green uniform of a colonel of the Pennsylvania Regiment and the other was Richard Grenough. Her eyes met with those of the wealthy merchant. He broke into a broad smile, nodded, and touched his hat to her. Then he said something to the colonel, and the two of them turned and walked off into the darkness.

* * *

Morning medical call was over. Munro turned to Mary. "I'm going over to see the adjutant; Lieutenant Welford says that another battalion of Pennsylvania Provincials is arriving today and they have a surgeon attached. He is supposed to tend both of the Pennsylvania battalions. Bouquet has the idea of consolidating his surgery with us for better efficiency and I'm supposed to discuss the idea with Welford."

Mary smiled. "Spend time with Lieutenant Welford, sir? I'm sure you'll enjoy that."

Munro gave Mary a tight-lipped glance. "Keep your thoughts on the officers to yourself, Mary."

"All right, I will. But I still don't have to like him. He's the most arrogant officer in in the Royal Americans."

"Be that as it may, he speaks for Bouquet." The surgeon motioned to all the items laid out for sick call. "You clean up and re-stow the supplies and implements."

Mary was at work when Timothy McGregor appeared at the end of the row of hospital tents. His left hand was heavily bandaged. He stood looking around the hospital area and then walked up to Mary. "I'm supposed to see Surgeon Munro this morning. He wanted to check my hand and replace the dressing."

"Well, Private McGregor, if you wanted to be seen by the surgeon, you should have been here over an hour ago." She gave him a look of impatience. "You may be new to the 42nd but you've been here long enough to know the hospital hours."

"My sergeant ordered me to do something before I came over here."

"A job for someone who obviously needs to go to medical call?" She motioned to the bandaged hand. "What sergeant would keep you busy when you need attention? Everyone knows how badly you burned your hand last night."

"Now lass, you don't know Sergeant Leslie of Stirling's Company."

Mary sighed. "All right, I'll take care of you, McGregor. Sit down in the chair beside that table."

McGregor looked askance at Mary and then glanced around the hospital tents. "Miss, you seem a wee bit young for this job. Where are the regular nurses?"

Mary felt a flash of anger. "Regular nurses? I'm near enough to seventeen. And I started helping my mother treat sick and wounded soldiers when I was ten. The first time a soldier died in my arms was when I was eleven. I was one of only three *regular* nurses at Bushy Run." She gave McGregor a withering look. "Now, Private McGregor, do you want a new dressing or don't you? I do have other things to attend to."

The youthful soldier blushed slightly and sat down in the chair and laid his hand on the table.

Mary untied the covering bandage and discarded the dressing. As she worked, she surreptitiously looked over the young highlander and what she saw confirmed her impression from the previous night. She had to admit he had a strong, handsome face, with a determined looking mouth, good teeth, fine nose, and wide-set blue eyes. He was tall, with muscular but graceful legs and arms.

With the dressing off, she inspected the burn. "You know those coals burned right down into the flesh, don't you?"

"Miss, you're 'na telling me anything I don't know, after trying to sleep with this last night."

She looked at him and said, "Well, you're going to have permanent scars. But you're lucky. The scars will only be on your palm and the underside of your fingers, so they won't be too visible. And I don't' think they'll be thick enough to interfere with using your hand."

McGregor nodded. "Now, I guess I'll be thankful for that."

Mary said, "Just so you know, I saw you fall into the fire last night. I found it surprising that you were able to keep from screaming. Not many men could have done that."

"A McGregor is brought up to keep his pain to himself."

Mary said nothing, concentrating on preparing a new cloth dressing. Then she said, "I'm going to put some ointment on the burned areas, McGregor. It's going to sting at first, but after that it will reduce the pain, at least for a while." She applied the ointment and then put the dressing in place. Finally, she wrapped the hand with a new bandage.

As she finished, Taggart came out of one of the tents where he had been working on morning reports. He walked over to the table and glanced down at Mary's work. Then he smiled and looked at the highlander. "You can consider yourself lucky that Mary was here to treat you. She's the best of our nurses; Munro says her work is as good as most surgeons." He paused and turned to Mary. "When you've finished with this man, will you please go in and check my figures on the morning report? You know how I always have trouble with my sums." Then he was off down the line of tents.

Mary looked the young highlander directly in the eyes and gave him her sweetest "I told you so" smile. "You're done, Private McGregor. You can go back to the tender mercies of your Sergeant Lester now."

McGregor looked sharply at Mary. "You can do sums?"

"Yes, Private McGregor; and I can also read and write. I was taught by Chaplin Ferguson of the 77th."

"Now why would a girl like you want to spend time learning all that? You'll not be needing it when you're married to a corporal or sergeant in a few years."

"I'll need reading and writing and doing my sums when I find a job as a tutor or a governess for a wealthy family's children. That's when!"

"You would leave the regiment?"

"This may surprise you, Private McGregor, but I don't want to spend all my life dressed in cast-off clothing and sleeping on the ground or on army cots. Someday I want to spend my nights in a real feather bed with real sheets. And eat meals at a proper table; food that I didn't have to cook myself." Mary started to gather up the medical implements and left-over dressing material. "And Private McGregor, the only way I know how to do that is to find a job in service with a good family after we get back to Scotland. That's where I see my future — not married to some corporal whose only object in life is to become a sergeant."

"You 'na have respect for sergeants?"

"My father was a sergeant." She pointed to an imposing hill which rose to the east of the fort. "He died on that hill trying to rally the 77th during Grant's Battle in '58. His grave is over there in the burial ground. So don't question me about respecting sergeants. And I've been with the army since I was seven. I watched my mother and stepfather — another sergeant — die of the fever in the West Indies back in '62. I've seen enough of the army to know that someday I want a different life."

McGregor looked at her silently for a moment, then stood up. "Thank you, Miss Fraser, for helping with my hand." Then he smiled down at her. "You're a wee slip of a girl; but full of a roaring great spirit, aren't you now?" A roguish look came over his face and a twinkle in his eyes. "I think it would be much better if you started calling me 'Tim' instead of Private McGregor, because I intend that you are going to be seeing a lot of me from now on."

And with that he touched a finger to his bonnet and was off, heading back to the camp of the 42nd.

Mary watched him go. He walked with a strong, confident stride and had something of a bounce in his step. She thought: *He is a saucy one and a bit full of himself, but the truth is, I wouldn't mind seeing more of this Timothy McGregor.*

CHAPTER TWO

The Scout

It was a slow afternoon in the hospital of the 42nd. The sun, well along toward the western horizon, was beginning to cast shadows from the tents, rows of stacked muskets, and wagons in the encampment around Fort Pitt. Mary and Kathryn were busy boiling cloth used for bandages and dressings. The great kettle was suspended over the fire on a tripod, and the nurses were taking turns stirring the contents with a long-handled paddle which allowed them to avoid most of the steam and the heat. Meanwhile, Surgeon Munro sat in his tent, paging through the thick new medical text he had received just before they left Carlisle. It had come all the way from London, and contained instructions for the newest medical procedures being practiced in Europe. A mug of libation sat beside his hand and the jug itself sat on the ground beside a table leg.

The two nurses had been making light-hearted conversation as they worked, but a natural pause had come over them. Thus in the momentary silence both of them heard the distant sound of massed drums at the same time. They looked at each other as they cocked their ears.

Kathryn said, "I reckon that's the new Pennsylvania battalion coming in."

Mary gave the pot a stir and nodded. She turned and looked over at the gap in the tree line where Forbes Road emerged from the forest. In a few seconds the battalion's mounted staff officers came into view, quickly followed by a band of massed fifes and drums drawn from the unit's companies. Then the first company, in column of fours, came into sight, with succeeding companies appearing from the tree line as the battalion marched up the road toward the fortress. She said, "They make a brave sight in their green uniforms, don't they?"

Munro rose from the table and walked, mug in hand, to where he could watch the column approach. Taggart and the two nurses joined him.

Taggart said, "Look, all the bigwigs are watching." He pointed to the bastion which towered above them.

Mary looked and saw several officers standing together in a group. She immediately recognized Bouquet, Colonel Reid of her own regiment, Mr. Grenough, and the Pennsylvania lieutenant colonel who had been watching her dance the night before. She turned to the surgeon. "Dr. Munro, beg your pardon, sir, but do you know the name of that Pennsylvania colonel up there?"

"Lass, that's Lieutenant Colonel Turbutt Francis, the commandant of the 1st Pennsylvania. Munro grinned slyly and leaned over close to her ear. He whispered, "He's the brother–in–law of Miss Nancy Willing, the woman who Bouquet was very openly courting in Philadelphia. Everyone thought their betrothal was all but certain. Then she suddenly married Turbutt's younger brother, Tench, while the colonel was out on campaign."

Mary looked at Munro. "It must have been very embarrassing for Bouquet."

"Yes, there were many sly comments and suppressed giggles in Philadelphia society. And think of the tension now for Bouquet to have to work every day with a man whose very presence is a reminder of the incident. I dare say, not very tactful of the Governor to have appointed Francis to the colonelcy."

"I'd say it's more like poking Bouquet in the eye with a stick." Mary said.

Munro looked askance at Mary. "You're again getting very close to showing lack of respect for your betters, lass."

Mary giggled to herself, then forced a look of contrition on her face. "Sorry, Dr. Munro; I really will try to do better."

Then she looked back at the Pennsylvania battalion as it approached their position on the glacis. In the distance, it had seemed impressive. But now, as the unit approached, her practiced military eyes led her to become more critical. While many of the men wore the green uniform coat, there were a significant number still dressed in civilian coats and breeches or hunting shirts and leggings. She also observed that the very marching of the battalion's men was noticeably ragged, lacking the precise, disciplined step and posture of British regulars. The soldiers had not mastered the right length of step and she could see several who were in fact out of step. The slope of the firelocks they carried was anything but uniform. There was also a mix of firearms; while most men carried muskets, there were a considerable number of riflemen present. And it seemed as if every man had interpreted the wearing of his hat in a slightly different way.

She leaned close to the surgeon. "I'd say Colonel Bouquet's going to have them spend some very serious time on the parade ground."

Munro looked at her and simply said, "Indeed."

Mary's eyes moved to the lieutenant colonel riding at the head of the battalion. He was dressed in a proper, well fitted uniform, brown hair tied in a cue under the tri-cornered black hat. He had a lean build and a pleasant, honest looking face.

He sat his big black horse with the easy elegance of a man who knows how to ride and has done a lot of it. Her glance moved to the men of the staff riding behind the colonel. And then her eyes lighted on a familiar figure. He was a lean, long-limbed, rangy man with a scruffy stubble beard. He was dressed in a fringed, undyed linen hunting shirt which reached about half-way down to his knees. Brown leggings covered his legs. A long rifle was slung over his shoulder, and on his head was a black, broad-brimmed hat with the right side turned up. Mary's heart skipped a beat.

Joshua! Joshua Baird!

Mary forgot military etiquette and instinctively called out "Joshua!"

Baird turned toward her; recognition flowed over his face and then his mouth broke into a great wide smile. He turned back and called out something to the colonel, who gave him a quick glance and then a wave of the hand. Then Baird pulled the head of his horse around, touched its flanks with his heels, and headed at the gallop directly for where Mary and the hospital staff stood. He pulled up his mount directly in front of Mary, and she instinctively ran out beside him. Baird reached down and took Mary's arm, and with an easy motion lifted her up and seated her sideways directly in front of his saddle.

Joshua smiled broadly, both eyes twinkling and said, "You ain't but a wee might heavier than when you was a little slip of a girl."

Mary twisted around and put her arms around Joshua. "I do feel like a little girl again. Oh Joshua, I'm so glad to see you. I wasn't sure you were going to come along on this expedition. Captain McDonald said you had gone with Wend to live in Virginia."

"Well, that I did, but nothin' was goin' to stop me from makin' this trip. And when it's over, I'm goin' by Carlisle and pick up the Widow Downy to live with us down near Winchester."

"Oh, you're finally going to make her an honest woman?"

Joshua smiled again. "Well, she don't know it yet, but I'm goin' to make a powerful argument to her." Then he lowered Mary to the ground and dismounted himself.

Mary said, "That's a right tall horse you've got there. And handsome looking."

"Well, this is what I've learned about Virginians since we got down there in June: They grow damned fine tobacco and breed strong horses that know how to run like the wind and jump high fences." He paused and patted the horse's black main. "This here bay's name is Beau, 'cause he does look so handsome." He paused and ran his hand over the horse's flank. "And so far, I ain't found the fence he couldn't take in his stride."

Meanwhile, Surgeon Munro had come over. He extended his hand to Joshua. "I feel a damn sight better knowing you're going to be scouting again, Joshua. You've been along on every campaign since '58. And no one knows the Ohio Country better than you."

Suddenly a strange voice asked from behind Joshua, "Sir, would your name happen to be Baird?"

Mary looked to see Colonel Bouquet's adjutant standing behind Joshua. The scout turned to look at the newcomer. "Aye, you got it, Lieutenant. Joshua Baird is the name."

"Permit me to introduce myself, sir. I am Lieutenant Reginald Welford of the 60th, and I have the honor to be adjutant to Colonel Bouquet."

Baird extended his hand. "Proud to meet you, Lieutenant."

Welford looked at Joshua as curiously as if he were some kind of newly discovered species and kept his own hands tightly by his sides. "Sir, the colonel extends his complements and requests that you wait upon him in his headquarters at your earliest convenience."

Joshua grinned. "Well, you tell the colonel I'll be right along, soon as I finish greeting my friends here and get my horse settled."

"Well, I'd say you should do that post haste. It would not do to keep Colonel Bouquet waiting." He paused and looked around. "Now I must be off to find Lieutenant Colonel Clayton of the Second Pennsylvania."

Joshua put his hand on Welford's shoulder and pointed to where the newly arrived troops were standing. "Lieutenant, you'll find old Asher over there, dismissing his men."

Welford recoiled from the scout's touch and said in a stern voice, "Mr. Baird, I would caution you to refer to officers of His Majesty's forces by their proper titles." Then he spun on his heel and marched off toward the Pennsylvania battalion as if on parade.

Baird's eyes followed the adjutant and then looked over at Munro. "Now ain't he somethin'? Pretty as the devil! And did you see all the fine needlework on his uniform and the lace on his shirt? Where did he come from?"

Munro smiled conspiratorially. "Lieutenant Welford came to the 60th directly from London. The word in the mess is that he managed to get himself thrown out of the Guards; something to do with gambling debts and indiscreetly chasing a major's young wife."

Joshua shook his head. "My, oh, my! He may find the border country rather interestin'."

The surgeon grinned broadly. "More interesting than he expects. Colonel Bouquet intimated to me that once we leave Fort Pitt, he's going to assign Welford to a line company. He'll be marching in the lead of a half-company with a pack on his back and carrying a fusil instead of riding a horse alongside Bouquet. That should open his eyes rather rapidly."

Baird looked after Welford and smiled. "Yes, indeed, that there lieutenant does need havin' his eyes opened." Then he turned back to Mary and took her hand. "I'll go along an' see Bouquet. But I'll come on back after dinner with a jug, and we'll sit by the fire, and I'll tell you about Wend."

Mary nodded and squeezed his hand back. "Yes, Joshua, I'd like that very much."

* * *

Later, just as Munro and Mary were finishing evening rounds — having visited the few men in the hospital — Taggart approached the surgeon. "Beg your pardon, sir, but the doctor from the Second Pennsylvania is here to see you."

Mary saw a middle-aged man of medium height, wearing a black coat and hat with gray breeches, who was standing near the surgeon's tent at the edge of the hospital. He had a lean build, but showed a bit of a paunch around his waist and wore spectacles over eyes which were busy scanning the lay-out of the hospital.

As they approached, the man made a slight bow and extended his hand to Munro. "I take it you are the surgeon of the 42nd, sir?"

"That I am, sir. Permit me to introduce myself; Surgeon Percy Munro, sir."

"Ah yes," said the other. "I am Doctor Charles Highsmith of Carlisle, sir. Currently under contract to the Pennsylvania Regiment."

"Well, Doctor, sit down here with me." The two men took places across the table in the tent and Munro introduced Taggart and Mary. Then he said to Highsmith, "I guess you have heard about Colonel Bouquet's idea to consolidate hospital operations?"

"Yes, in fact that's why I'm here. A young, very cheeky lieutenant told me — rather peremptorily, I might add — to come see you about us working together. I'm certainly not opposed to the idea; share the workload and all that."

"Precisely, sir,' responded Munro. He screwed up his face. He said quietly "Let me be very tactful about this, Dr. Highsmith: Colonel Bouquet also thought it might be beneficial for me to help you learn to treat the type of wounds we might see in action against the savages."

Highsmith leaned back in his chair and sat silent for a moment. Then he raised an eyebrow and said very slowly, "Well, I do take your meaning, Doctor Munro."

Mary had been watching Highsmith very closely, and saw that, while he was becoming irritated at Munro's condescending tone, he was doing a good job of keeping his feelings under control.

Munro continued, "Good, sir. Now, as a doctor in practice in Carlisle, I presume that you have not had any experience in military surgery on the field of action?"

Highsmith slowly adjusted his glasses, then stared beyond Munro as if he were considering what to say. Shortly, he crossed his arms in front of his chest and answered, almost reluctantly, "Quite right, sir, I must admit that I've had no *military* experience." He drew out the word military as if to emphasize it.

"Ah, Highsmith, there you are! There you are, indeed! That's my point precisely. Now let me assure you, I'll be glad to show you some techniques we use here for the rapid removal of limbs and the expeditious treatment of other types of wounds."

Highsmith leaned forward. "I'll be very glad for that, Doctor Munro. Of course, the fact is I have removed quite a few limbs myself under less than ideal conditions."

"Yes? And how did that happen to occur? I wouldn't have thought you would have seen much of that kind of work in Carlisle."

Highsmith replied with a deadpan face, "You're quite right, Munro. It actually occurred during my service as surgeon of HMS Falmouth, 50, and HMS Minerva, 32 during the late war, sir. And naturally, in that kind of service I also treated numerous wounds from balls and splinters. Of course, that wasn't in the *field*, as you put it, sir. But it was in the rather cramped space of a ship's cockpit, operating by the light of lanterns, with blood puddled on the deck and groaning men lying about waiting for their turn on the table."

Mary quickly put her hand to her mouth to keep from giggling. Seeing the expression on Munro's face was worth a day's ration.

The surgeon of the 42nd reared back in his chair and then half rose from his seat, his jaw set, his face red. "Why sir, you have been making sport at my expense. Sport, by God! I asked if you had any military experience and you denied it. Damn sir, you have been leading me on!"

Highsmith raised his eyebrows. "Sir, you most clearly asked if I had *military* experience. And indeed I answered you truthfully. In fact, I have had only *naval* experience." He leaned forward and smiled roguishly. "You will of course admit that the two words do mean different things?"

The two men sat rigidly staring at each other for a long moment. Then Munro's face relaxed, he cleared his throat, and turned to a cabinet. He pulled out two mugs and a jug and placed them on the table. Then the surgeon grinned broadly. "Well, Doctor Highsmith, it occurs to me that the sun is rather low on the horizon. Perhaps you would care to take a bumper with me and we could discuss setting up our joint surgery."

"Why Doctor Munro, nothing would give me greater pleasure."

* * *

Mary and Joshua sat in front of the hospital fire. Other people were sitting on the other side, but the two sat alone in quiet conversation, catching up with each other. Mary had her arms around Joshua's right arm and her head on his shoulder, her eyes staring into the flames. In low tones, the scout was telling her about Wend Eckert. He had explained how they had all thought she was dead and how Wend had returned to the home of his step-parents in Sherman Valley after the prior year's campaign. He told her about Wend's marriage to Peggy McCarty, the daughter of Sherman Mill's tavern keeper. Mary asked, "I heard about that from Captain McDonald. But how was it that Wend left Pennsylvania for Virginia?"

"It be a long story, lass. But to make it short, Mary, he shot some men who were illegally trading with the Ohio tribes and were also responsible for inciting the murder of the Conestoga Indians near Lancaster. Wend knew people in the tribe from when he lived there, particularly the family of his friend Charlie Sawak. So he vowed to take revenge and he was able to shoot the men along Forbes Road while they were on their way to provide arms to the hostile war parties. Then the men's boss —a man of great influence in the colony — began pressing the sheriff of Cumberland County to arrest Wend. So the day after they were married, Wend took Peggy and left for Virginia. Donegal and I went with them to help make the journey and help set them up in a homestead."

Mary looked up at Joshua. "Captain McDonald said that he told Wend and you that I was still alive when you stopped at Fort Loudoun."

"Yes, and Wend took it very hard. Mary, it's certain that he's still in love with you. When we walked out of the fort, he had to brace himself against the stockade wall to keep from collapsing at the trick fate had played on the two of you. Donegal wanted him to write you to explain what had happened. But Wend decided that would only upset you."

"Yes, I can understand. The fact is, that's why I didn't try to get in touch with Wend after you all got back from the Ohio Country. I thought he would be with Abigail and I didn't want to interfere with their life." She sighed. "It was all a great misunderstanding; but now it's done and can't be fixed, Joshua."

"Yes, and now Peggy has a baby on the way."

They both looked into the fire for a long time, the two of them lost in thought.

Then Mary said, with an air of whimsy, "Joshua, I wish you had been able to marry my Mum back in '58, like I know you wanted to do after father was killed in Grant's Battle. If you had, we'd have gotten out of the army and Mum would still be alive. She wouldn't have died from fever in the West Indies. I used to dream about the three of us living in a cabin in the woods somewhere. And then I would have never met Wend and our lives would have followed another course. Maybe that would have been better for everyone."

"Lass, you know I was away on a long scout when your Pa was killed. I would have married Lizzie in a heartbeat. But your Ma had no way of knowing that I would have asked her. So she had to marry Sergeant Iverson to make sure you and she stayed on the ration roll."

Mary shrugged. "Yes, I know. Well, the truth is, we can't go back and make things right."

Joshua looked down at the girl. "What will you do now? Word is the 42nd will be ordered back to Scotland soon and you'll have to make a decision."

"There are men who come around and want to marry me. But I'll not accept. I'm staying with my plan. I'll leave the regiment and go into service with a family — here or in Scotland. The chaplain says he'll help me with references."

After that, conversation languished. Baird became increasingly quiet, staring into the fire for long periods. He took long pulls on the jug which he had brought. Mary, knowing the scout, found the moodiness strange, for he was normally full of stories and laughter, particularly when stimulated by drink. Finally, she asked straight-out, "What's on your mind, Joshua?"

Baird bit his lip, as if trying decide what to say. "Well, Mary I got a problem. I got to do something what's real hard, and I ain't sure how to go about it."

"What kind of thing is it?"

"I need to tell Bouquet that he's got a traitor riding with the expedition."

Mary looked at him with astonishment written all over her face. "My God! A traitor? How can that be?" She thought a minute. "Come on Joshua, how do you know?"

Baird looked at her and raised an eyebrow. "I know 'cause Wend found it out."

Mary's jaw dropped. "Wend? I don't understand."

"He discovered it while he was tracking down those Indian traders he killed. This man is the very leader of their ring; the man who forced Wend out of Pennsylvania. This man is behind the tribes getting the powder and lead they've needed to carry out their war. He also influenced the Paxton Militia to massacre the Conestogas, and then he helped stir up the Ulster people to ride against Philadelphia. All of that was to distract from his trading with the Indians. Truth be known, this man is responsible for much of the death we've seen in this uprising."

"Why is it so hard to tell Bouquet, Joshua?"

"Because there ain't no hard evidence. The man has covered his tracks pretty well. And most of what hard evidence there was, like the gunpowder, lead, and hatchet's that was going to the Indians — was destroyed by Wend when he shot those two scoundrels on Forbes Road. So all I got is my word to Bouquet. But the man has got to be stopped, or he'll do it all over again and more people will die."

"Bouquet trusts you; you and he have been working together since he came to Pennsylvania six years ago. He will believe what you tell him and figure out how to stop the traitor."

"Yes, but I have to be careful. There ain't no way Bouquet can get this man arrested and punished under the law. All he can do is find a way to cut him out of influencing the colony and carrying out trade with the tribes. Perhaps he can ruin his reputation with the governor. And this is what's particularly botherin' me: If Bouquet really hurts him bad enough, the traitor has the power to reach right into Virginia and take retribution against Wend."

"God, you can't let that happen!" Mary pondered for a moment. "Who is this man?"

Joshua shook his head. "No, I ain't tellin' you Mary. I ain't tellin' anyone but Bouquet. I don't want you to be involved in any way. This man is too dangerous and it's better if you honestly don't know anything. I probably told you too much already."

Mary shrugged. "So, what are you going to do?"

"I got to get it straight in my mind what to say to the colonel and the proper time to tell him. Maybe as the campaign goes on somethin' will come up that will give me the right opportunity. I figure that's all I can do."

There was another long silence. Then Mary changed the subject. "When will the expedition get started, Joshua? Did Bouquet tell you when you called on him?"

"Bouquet's had men busy building rafts and collecting boats. All the units from Virginia and Pennsylvania are here now. There's still some more companies from Maryland coming, but the colonel ain't waiting for them; they'll catch up with us on the march. The army will begin crossing the Allegheny on the first day of October."

Mary said, "That's less than a week from now!"

Joshua nodded. "Yes, but Bouquet wishes we were already deep into the Ohio Country. Fact is, he wanted to start the expedition in June or even earlier and have the whole thing all wrapped up by now. But the provincial governments, particularly those damned Quakers in Philadelphia, dragged their feet over raising the troops and paying for them. So now we are not only facing the tribes but also the comin' of the cold and stormy weather. If we get trapped by the snow out in that Ohio forest, we'll be in a real pickle. That's got Bouquet worried mightily."

Mary nodded. "We've already had some very cold nights."

"Yes, and it ain't goin' to do anything but get worse. But the fact is, it will be busy between now and when we start the crossing. Bouquet plans to use the time drilling all the provincial troops. Moreover, he's made up the plan for a marching formation which he thinks will make it almost impossible for the tribes to stage an ambush. He'll be holding meetings with the senior officers to explain it to them and tell them their duties."

Mary waved back toward the troop camps around them. "These provincials need every bit of training they can get, Joshua."

Joshua smiled. "That's true enough." He thought a moment. "Once we get across the Allegheny and head for the Muskingum River, I'm to ride with the Virginia riflemen under Major John Field. They'll be leading the advance." He thought for a moment. "We got more than 1200 men, not counting the contractors and drovers. Bouquet hopes it's enough to convince the tribal kings not to make a fight."

"Do you think he's right?"

"Might be, but only time will tell. The fact is, Mary, we'll only know the answer when we start pushing into the Ohio Country."

CHAPTER THREE
The Advance

The army began its movement precisely on schedule. Bouquet had assembled a flotilla of boats — bateaux, rafts, canoes — to ferry the force across the Allegheny. The initial unit to cross, elements of Major John Field's Virginia rangers, took to their boats at dawn on the first day of October. The riflemen landed at the site of the abandoned Indian village which had been built in the prior year during the siege of Fort Pitt and lay directly across from the fort. Field, with Joshua Baird heading a group of scouts, quickly led his men in a sweep of the village, and then set up defensive positions to shield the landings from an attack, unlikely as that might seem. Baird and his scouts then ranged ahead down to the Ohio, sweeping the forest and searching for a proper site for the first camp.

Behind the riflemen and scouts came the trickiest and most time consuming movement of the crossing — swimming the huge herd of pack horses, sheep, and cattle across the wide river. The total of sheep and bullocks alone amounted to over 800 animals. In addition to that were several hundred pack horses. The animals were segmented into groups of manageable size and moved across in phased echelons, shepherded by drovers in boats. The loaded packs were brought over in rafts and large bateaux. The crossing of the entire pack train and herd took two days.

The movement of the main force of troops was accomplished on the third of October in a phased, tightly scheduled operation. The first group of boats brought over Bouquet's headquarters and the hospital. The hospital equipage had been stripped down to the necessities to require the minimum number of packhorses, as had Bouquet's headquarters baggage. There would be no wagons on the expedition, for the only routes through the vast Ohio Country were trails and streams. Moreover, if combat ensued, the colonel didn't want his ability to maneuver constrained by a slow moving wagon train.

seventeen miles down the Ohio, near the mouth of the Beaver River. I hope we can make about half that distance in the first day. I expect the slowness of the bullock and sheep herd will limit us to about ten miles a day."

As they were talking, Mary finished with Grenough's hand. She looked up and saw that Joshua had arrived. He was leaning against the front post of the Doctors' tent with his firelock grounded in front of him, watching the proceedings.

Grenough saw Baird at almost the same time. He called out, "Well hello, Joshua. I assume you have some news for us?"

Bouquet looked around and saw the scout. "Ah, yes, Joshua — are you bringing me some word from Major Field?"

"That's a fact, colonel. We got pickets set up on the landward side of the village and roving patrols screening the troops as they move down to the campsite. But the real news is we sighted our first bunch of warriors."

Bouquet pursed his lips. "I presume they were here to keep an eye on us?"

"Yep, Colonel; I saw them myself and made them out to be Kispoko Shawnees. That clan is tough fighters and they pride themselves in their scoutin'. But they was pretty brazen and didn't make no real effort to hide themselves. It was clear they was tryin' to feel us out, see how we'd react."

"Major Field didn't attack, did he? I didn't hear any firing."

"Naw', Colonel — he made sure everybody held their fire and just watched the Shawnees. After a few minutes them Redskins disappeared into the woods."

"Excellent, Joshua. Give my compliments to John. That's just how I wanted him to handle it. I want the tribal leaders to know we're on our way."

Joshua nodded. "Well, you can bet they'll be war parties hangin' around, sendin' messages to their chiefs all along our line of march."

"Yes, I want them to see our strength. I'm particularly glad those were Shawnee. Of all the tribes, their leaders are the most inclined to fight. If they see how many men we have, that may temper their enthusiasm." Bouquet turned back to Grenough. "Richard, when you get done here, come on over to my tent. Ensign Hutchins has laid out a map and we can consider our route."

With that he was off back to the headquarters, Joshua walking with him.

Grenough looked around at the hospital. "They seem to have stripped you down to the bare essentials."

Mary nodded. "Colonel Bouquet said we could only bring along the two doctors, two orderlies, and two of the nurses. We left several nurses behind at Pitt. And the main reason he allowed any nurses along was to help take care of female and children hostages which the Indians may release as part of the treaty negotiations."

The merchant smiled. "Well, Miss Fraser, it speaks well of you that they chose someone so young to accompany the expedition."

Mary smiled at Grenough. "Sir, I may be just going on seventeen, but I've been nursing since I was eleven. So despite my age, I've had a lot of experience. I was at Ticonderoga and Bushy Run."

Doctor Munro had come over while they were talking. "Mary is indeed one of my most experienced nurses. And she took a ball last year at Bushy Run which nearly cost her life."

Grenough's eyes opened wide and he seemed to look at her with new eyes. "Well, you are a proper soldier, aren't you?" Then he smiled mischievously. "May I be so bold as to say that I wish all our soldiers were as pretty and enchanting as you, Miss Fraser?"

* * *

The staff of the hospital watched all day as the boat flotilla shuttled the army across the Allegheny. There were a few casualties as the day went on which were handled expeditiously. Then they packed their gear onto horses and marched with the last company down to the first camp where they again set up their tents and held evening medical call.

At dusk, Kathryn came up to Mary, who was repacking supplies for the next day's march. A wide grin was on her face. "That boy from Stirling's Company who burned his hand is here to have the dressing changed and the wound inspected. He says you told him to come directly to you."

Mary stood up and frowned. "Sure I told him no such thing. Tell him I'm busy and that you can do it just as well as me."

Kathryn laughed. "He'll 'na take that for an answer." She cocked her head with a knowing grin on her face. "It's sure he's got other things on his mind and he's a determined lad indeed. If he's to be discouraged in his pursuit, he'll take the word only from you." She paused a moment and looked back at the front of the hospital. "Besides, you've got to admit, he's 'na so bad to look on and he's got a nice twinkle in his eyes."

"Well, twinkle or not, he'll have to wait a while." Mary deliberately finished what she was doing, which took nearly ten minutes, then walked, in an unhurried way, to where McGregor stood beside the main treatment tent.

The highlander smiled broadly and touched his bonnet to her. "And how are you this fine evening, Miss Mary?"

Mary ignored the greeting. She pointed to the table and chair under the tent's canopy and said peremptorily, "Sit there and put your hand on the table, Private McGregor." While he complied, she busied herself gathering up ointment and new dressing cloth.

When she returned to the table, he said, "Now aren't you forgetting my name is Tim? That would be so much easier than all that repeating 'Private McGregor' over and over."

Mary ignored him. "Your hand is doing much better. It has healed well over the last week. This will probably be the last dressing we'll have to put on you." She looked closely at his palm. "Come back after tomorrow's march and we'll remove the dressing and take a final look at your hand."

"So soon?" McGregor shook his head. "Then I'll be havin' to find new reasons to come visit you, won't I?"

Mary had to work hard to keep from smiling at the youth's determination. She finished tying the bandage, then looked at him sternly. "Now look: You can visit me all you want, or at least as much as your sergeant will let you. And after hours, I'll be pleasant company. But remember what I told you: I'm not going to marry a soldier and I'm leaving the army. There's many other men who have come visiting me and some have even fought over me. But it didn't improve them in my graces or change my mind one bit."

"Now you try to be the hard one, don't you Mary? But I'm thinkin' the right man could soften that look on your face."

"I've already met the right man. But the Lord took him from me. So I'm intent on carrying out my plan."

"Ah, now, there can be more than one right man for you, Mary. Particularly if the first man you loved is dead. And I'm thinkin' I could be that man."

"He's not dead. He's married to another woman." She looked at McGregor with as steely a face as she could manage. "And now it's time for you to get back to your company, Timothy McGregor, before Sergeant Leslie finds cause to brace you up against a tree and give you a touch of his hand." She turned and stocked off toward the rear of the hospital. McGregor shouted after her, "Well, you called me 'Timothy' that time. I'm thinking we're makin' progress, lass!"

It took all Mary's willpower not to look back at the young soldier.

* * *

In the gathering dusk, Mary walked the short distance from the hospital to the group of tents which housed the headquarters of the 42nd, a sheaf of papers in her hand. Around her, the encampment was a beehive of activity. Troops were putting the final touches on their campsites for the night. Every company was building barricades using loaded pack saddles from the supply train, for Bouquet had decreed that the expedition's camp would be fortified every night. There was a cacophony of other sounds. Mary could hear mooing of the cattle and bleating of sheep from the herd, sergeants shouting at their squads, the tramp of marching detachments. She had to stop and wait as the men of a light horse troop led their mounts out to a picket line on the periphery of the camp.

She soon came to the tent of Chaplain MacLagen. He was new to the Black Watch, having just recently joined the battalion. He had eagerly agreed to continue the work of the former chaplain, Ferguson, who had been Mary's long time mentor, tutor, and guardian in lieu of actual family. The chaplain was sitting on a camp chair in front of his tent, taking in the scene. He saw Mary and smiled broadly. "Ah, it's good to see you lass."

"I've brought you my lessons, Mr. MacLagen. I did the sums and the subtractions."

"Excellent, Mary." MacLagen took the papers. "I will review your work as soon as I can." Then he motioned her to wait and went into his tent. Soon he emerged with a paper in his hand. "Here is your new lesson, Mary. Another set of mathematical problems for you to solve."

Mary took the paper. "I'll do them as soon as I can, sir. But I think there won't be a lot of time now that we'll be on the march."

MacLagen nodded. "Do the best you can." Then he shook his head. "I'm sorry to say, I don't have any new reading for you. I had to leave most of my baggage behind at Pitt, per orders to keep things as light as possible. All my books except the Bible are back there."

Mary shrugged. "That's all right, sir. Surgeon Munro's got a new medical book which he brought along. He's letting me read that, and it's got a lot of new words for me to figure out. And I'm learning a lot more about medicine as I go along."

"Excellent, Mary; I feel relieved that you will have some challenging material to keep your mind occupied." He paused a moment, then said, "By the way, I have some exciting information for you."

"Really, sir? What would that be?"

"Mr. Richard Grenough, the wealthy merchant who is advising Colonel Bouquet on Indian affairs, visited with the mess of the 42nd today. He mentioned you to me; he was quite impressed with your skill when you treated him this morning for the splinter in his hand. He was also taken with your intelligence and vocabulary." MacLagen beamed at Mary. "He said it was immediately clear to him that you weren't the typical camp girl."

Mary said, "I'm a little surprised he said that; the truth is, we had just a very short conversation while I worked on him."

MacLagen said, "Well, when I told him that I was working with you, he became very enthusiastic. He pulled me aside and asked for more information about you. I told him about your aspirations to become a children's governess and tutor, and how dedicated you were to learning." MacLagen smiled. "And he was very interested in that. But here's the main point; he suggested that he might be able to help you obtain a position if you decided to stay here in the colonies."

Mary felt a thrill. But it was immediate tempered by a sobering thought. "He said that? Do you think he *really* meant it? Perhaps he was just trying to make polite conversation."

"Mary, in my position I must be a good judge of men. And in my opinion, he was clearly sincere. And most importantly for you, he pointed out that he knew well-off families in Philadelphia, New York, and even Williamsburg. He said undoubtedly there were positions for bright young girls like you who could fit in with a cultured home." He paused a second. "Of course, that would mean staying here in the colonies. Perhaps you have your heart set on going back to Scotland?"

Mary shook her head. "I have no really close family back there to draw me. So I could be happy here. The position is more important than the location."

"Capital, my dear!" MacLagen grinned broadly. "Now all you have to do is remain in Mr. Grenough's good graces throughout the campaign and I'm sure he would be willing to draft a letter of reference for you and perhaps even arrange introductions to possible employers."

Mary left the chaplain's tent feeling a surge of excitement. *Was it possible that her long time dreams were about to come true? That a chance meeting would open the door to a new life?* She walked back to the hospital in the glow of high spirits.

* * *

The next morning the drums beat reveille well before dawn. The morning meal was hurriedly completed, tents were struck, packhorses loaded. The night before, Munro had told the hospital staff that Bouquet intended to order practice drills before the expedition began its march and consequently required that all routine morning matters be dealt with by the time daylight had arrived.

By the time the drummers began beating the General Call all the elements of the army were in their assigned positions within the marching formation. As Joshua had told Mary, Bouquet had designed a formation which provided defense in depth for the passage through hostile territory. Now, in the growing light, she could see the placement of all the units.

Munro stood in front of the hospital staff, a piece of paper in his hands. "Now pay attention; here is how we shall make our way through the wilderness." He turned and pointed to the very front of the column. "A detachment of Virginia riflemen and the guides will range well ahead of the formation. Behind them will be a force of axe-men, made up of all the artificers and protected by the light infantry. Also with them will be a small group of light horse." He looked down and consulted the paper. "The axe-men will clear three parallel trails. The rest of the army will move along those trails in a long box-like formation. The front face of the box will consist of a company of the 42nd, which will form a line across all three paths. The rest of the 42nd will form the right side of the box in single file, on the outer trail on that side. The left side will be formed by a file of the 60th and the 1st Pennsylvania. Headquarters, the reserve ammunition, the officer baggage, the provisions train and we of the hospital will follow in the center trail." He pointed to the soldiers who stood on either side of the hospital. "We can mark our proper station by the location of the two grenadier companies; the 42nd on the right and the 60th on the left. They will form the expedition's reserve and our immediate protection."

Mary looked at the specially selected tall, burly soldiers who made up the elite grenadier company of each regiment and felt reassured that the hospital would be marching with them. "After the reserve, the 2nd Pennsylvania will form both sides of the box. Following us will be the two herds; first the bullocks and then the sheep. Behind them will be the brigades of pack horses with general supplies."

Munro pointed to the rear of the column. "The rearguard will be provided by a company of the 2nd Pennsylvania, another group of light horse, and a detachment of Virginia riflemen." Then he pointed to groups of riflemen standing outside the actual formation. "The Virginians will also provide parties of flankers, ranging through the forest at some distance from the convoy, to provide warning of the approach of any enemy party."

The surgeon had just finished speaking when Mary saw Colonel Bouquet riding along the formation, accompanied by Lieutenant Colonels Reid and Francis.

He pulled up near them and pointed to the lines of soldiers which formed the outer faces of the box. Then he spoke to the captain of the 42nd Grenadiers. "Sir, the general order specifies six feet between men of the outer files. Your men are too close together. See that they maintain the proper distance and keep silent as they march, their eyes outward. Permit no gap between the end of your company and the beginning of the first company of Pennsylvanians. Do not allow your men to let their guard down!" Then he was off further down the lines, talking with each company commander in turn.

Shortly, Bouquet and his companions rode back up to the head of the column. Almost immediately, drums began signaling "To Arms." Munro said, "Bouquet told us last night that he would exercise the command in the formation to receive the enemy if we are ambushed. That's the signal for all the companies to assume defensive positons."

Mary watched as officers waved the units of the train to tighten up and then reform from a column into a compact box. At the same time the line companies began assuming double ranks and maneuvering to form a huge square around the units of the train.

Munro said, "We're lucky; being already in the center, we merely have to remain in our position and everybody else closes up around us." As he spoke, the grenadier companies completed taking position within the box in their role as the force reserve.

Mary noticed that, while the grenadiers formed quickly, other companies — particularly the provincials — had trouble determining their proper stations. In fact, there was considerable confusion throughout the formation. Soon members of Bouquet's staff came riding down the lines, shouting at the captains and motioning the units into their correct locations.

Doctor Highsmith was taking in the maneuvers with a grin on his face. He turned to Munro and said dryly, "Obviously Bouquet knew his business in calling for the drill. This damn well looks as confused as the first time a newly commissioned ship beats to quarters — pandemonium all around!"

Munro shook his head. "Yes, I've no doubt we'll be practicing this again tomorrow morning. I wager the company commanders will face a rather bracing critique from the colonel this evening."

After all the units had finally found their place, the drums beat "Recall" and the army resumed its marching formation. Then the signal for the advance was beat, the bagpipes began their wail, and the expedition finally began its march, having consumed over an hour in the practice session.

It took a while to get all the elements of the long column fully into motion, but soon enough the convoy was moving at a deliberate pace through the dense, all-enveloping forest.

* * *

Surgeon Munro examined Private Timothy McGregor's hand while Mary held a lantern to provide adequate light. The expedition had had just finished making camp, after advancing only eight miles on their first day of marching. Then, since it was the first field camp of the campaign, Bouquet had taken another hour to personally supervise the precise layout of all units and the packsaddle breastworks. Thus evening routine had not even started until dusk was well upon them.

Now Munro nodded as he looked at McGregor's burn in the flickering light from the lantern. "Well, Private, you're a lucky man. The scaring has healed very well and is light enough so that you've got full use of that hand and fingers. But we want to be careful." He looked up at Mary. "We don't need any dressing, but give him a bandage to keep over the hand for the next few days to protect the scaring."

After Munro had left, Mary put the lantern on the table and sat down. "All right, McGregor, give me your hand and I'll wrap it."

"Ah now, that's my great pleasure, Mary, to have you holdin' my hand. But it's concernin' to me that you're back to calling me by 'McGregor' again. I thought we had it all settled that I was 'Tim'."

Mary shook her head. "All right, *Tim*; do you always prattle on like that?"

"It's one of a soldier's few pleasures to talk to a pretty lass. And I'll 'na be wastin' any of the short time I have with you by sittin' here silent."

Mary shrugged. "Well, I can't stop you."

"Ah, lass, there's plenty to say tonight. I've learned a lot about you in the last day. Now I know about this German fellow Eckert who was courting you on the last campaign. And why you aren't married to the lad." He looked her in the eye. "Tragic thing it was, but it's my good luck."

She said sternly, "I'm beginning to see that you think you can poke around into other people's business. And if you had done a better job, you'd know that it all began because I pursued him, not because of him coming to court me. And you're not going to have any luck with me."

"You pursued the man? Now what would it be takin' to get you to pursue me?"

"A miracle, Private McGregor."

Undeterred, McGregor continued, "I also found out the details about how your father became a true hero to the men of the old 77th. And because of what he did, every man of that regiment looked over you like you were his own little sister." He paused and smiled. "It's good for me that most of them have gone home, or I'd have them looking over my shoulder every time I came to see you."

Mary shook her head. "Right now, I wish some of them were around to grab you by your collar and drag you back to your company."

"Well, maybe before you call the lads to take me away, you'll look at what I've got here under my jacket." He pulled out a paper.

Mary was surprised. "Why, that's a copy of the Pennsylvania Gazette!"

"Indeed it is; and a recent one at that. I picked it up after one of the swells at headquarters threw it away. After I finished reading it, I thought you would want to see it, you bein' so interested in learnin' and what's goin' on in the world these fine days."

Mary looked at the young highlander. "You can read?"

A look of triumph came over McGregor's face. He read the top sentence of one story. "Now Miss Mary, are you thinkin' you're the only one in the regiment who can ken the written word? Do you 'na think others have had some schoolin'?"

Mary was somewhat taken aback. "It's not every soldier who can read." She took the newspaper from McGregor and gave him a grateful smile. "It was very thoughtful for you to bring it to me."

Tim McGregor stood up and touched his bonnet to Mary. He grinned broadly. "I'm glad to see we're getting' on so well in such a short time. I'll be back to see you in a day or two when I don't have the guard. Perhaps we can sit down together and read some of the stories, like I'm told you used to do with that fellow Eckert. I'm thinkin' you'll find me just as good company as he was."

* * *

Kirkwood appeared at the hospital fire just after they had finished the evening meal. Mary was seated across the coals from Taggart and Lister, who was Doctor Highsmith's orderly. The two men were sharing a small jug of rum and Mary had had a couple of sips to help dispel the chill of the night.

Mary saw that the corporal was carrying a bundle of clothing. "What have you got there, Bob? Somebody want me to do their wash?"

Kirkwood dropped the clothing into Mary's lap. "Better than that, lass; I've got a good piece of work for you; sewing that's needed as fast as you can do it."

Mary held the clothing up to the light of the fire. It was a collection of officer uniform parts, which she examined closely, rubbing her hand across the cloth. She held up a coat. "Bob, this is made of exceedingly fine material. The best I've ever seen. Where did you get it?"

"I'll have you know that is the uniform of his lordship the high and once very mighty Lieutenant Welford, formerly of the Guards and late adjutant of Colonel Bouquet himself. However, startin' today he's an ordinary lieutenant in Captain Stirling's company." Kirkwood smiled wickedly. "At this very moment he's out in the darkness of the bush standing duty in charge of camp guards."

Mary grinned "I can't think of a better place for him." Then she wrinkled up her face in puzzlement. "But what is Welford doing in the Black Watch? He's from the 60th."

"Colonel Bouquet seconded him to the 42nd, specifically to serve under Stirling. The rumor is that he figured Mr. Welford would take orders better from someone high-born like Stirling rather than your run of the mill Royal American officer." He shook his head. "Anyway, we got him for the rest of this campaign. And the first thing Captain Stirling did was tell Welford to get one of his uniforms fixed up for service here in the bush."

Mary held up a long-tailed uniform coat. She felt irritated just thinking about the arrogant English officer. "So why should I do all this for that ass Welford?"

Kirkwood reached out and took Mary's right hand. Then he dumped a collection of coins into her palm. "Now lassie, these should be good enough reason."

Mary quickly counted the coins. She looked up at Kirkwood and raised an eyebrow. "It's twice what is normal for this kind of work."

The corporal grinned broadly. "Now how would the good Mr. Welford know that? He asked me what it would cost, and I, thinking of you, lass, gave him a figure; a figure which he readily handed over."

Mary looked askance at Kirkwood and then broke into a wide grin. "Bob, you are a born scoundrel." Then she had another thought. "And how much did you keep for yourself, Bob?"

Kirkwood smiled, "Just a tiny amount; a wee bit of it for finding the work, as you might say."

The two orderlies had been taking all this in. Taggart laughed and said, "Mary, don't be worried about getting' all that money; take what you can from that dandy. Lord knows he can afford it and you can use it!"

Mary looked back at Kirkwood. "So what do you want done?"

"I want you to fix up the uniform like the 60th does when they're in the field. Take the sleeves off the long coat and sew them onto the waistcoat. That'll be what Welford wears as his outer coat here on campaign. Take care you don't damage the long coat; he'll carry that in his baggage and slip it over the waistcoat on cold days and at night, for extra warmth. And remove any lace or anything else which would show that Welford's an officer. Stirling said he didn't want him to be a target for an Indian sharpshooter."

Taggart elbowed Lister and cracked, "Pity that; I think he'd make a choice target. It would save us all a lot of grief if some buck put a ball into him!"

Kirkwood reached down and picked up the officer's tri-cornered hat. "Cut the threads which hold up the brim on this and make it into a wide-brimmed hat; then trim about an inch off the brim all around; you've seen the way the 60th wear their hats out here in the bush."

"That's no problem." Then Mary reached down and picked up a pair of tan breeches, made of cheap, coarse material. "What do you want me to do with these?"

"I got those from the quartermaster. They're left over from last year's campaign when Bouquet had the 42nd and 77th in breaches and leggings instead of kilts. They're for Welford to wear on the march. I took his measurements and I've pinned them in places so you can cut them down to fit him."

Mary collected all the clothing, rolled the items into a ball, and plunked them down beside her. Then she looked up at Kirkwood and pointed her finger at him. "Bob, why have you been telling Timothy McGregor about my past?"

"Now, lass, what do you mean by that?"

"You know damn well what I mean. He came over here today and knew everything about me."

Kirkwood shook his head. "Now, now, Mary, any of the old crowd from the 77th could have told him about you."

"Tell the truth, Bob."

"Come on, my sweet lassie, sure and the lad's got a case for you. And he's a fine strapping man; all the company likes him. And he's just the right age for you." He shook his head. "Now listen to me: Its time you started thinkin' of someone else besides Eckert. You can't spend all your life moonin' over him — you'll end up a spinster. And that would be a perfect tragedy."

"Bob, you know I have a plan; I have ambitions. Wend was an accident; a wonderful accident, but one I'm not going to allow to happen again."

"Yes, everyone knows how you've been thinkin'; but you're gettin' old enough to face the truth: no camp girl is going to get hired into some fine, rich house to teach the master's little brats." Kirkwood sighed. "Mary, I love you to death, just like every other man of the old 77th, but your dream — that's 'na goin' to happen."

Mary felt a spark of anger and an irresistible urge to strike back. She gritted her teeth. "That shows how much you know, Robert Kirkwood. The fact is I have a prospect this very instant."

Kirkwood cocked his head and froze, staring down at her. "Now Mary, that's a foolish thing to say. How can that be, with us out here on campaign in the middle of this bloody wilderness? I'm sorry if I hurt your feelings, but it's embarrassing to see you make up somethin' like that."

Mary almost blurted out the story about Grenough, but realized it would be indiscreet to tell anyone about his offer. Instead she said, "You still that tongue of yours, Bob. What I'm telling you is true enough. It is *true*, do you understand? The chaplain is working on something for me; something right here in the colonies. Scotland or England isn't the only place a position can be had."

Kirkwood shrugged, then said, "I still don't ken how he could be doing that for you in the middle of the bush; but then he's a new man and maybe he has connections, as they say." Then he stopped abruptly, lost in thought. Finally his face brightened and he said, "Unless, Mary, he's talking with someone here with the expedition. Is it one of the officers — from the Pennsylvania or Virginia regiments — who is makin' an offer to you?"

Mary shook her head. "I'm not telling you any more, Robert Kirkwood. Not another thing! Besides, it's time for you to be going back to your company. Come back in two days' time and I'll have Mr. Welford's sewing done. That's the best I can do with us on the march like this, and he can consider himself lucky at that."

Kirkwood smiled. "Two days it is; that's fair enough, lass. I'll be around just before lights out the day after tomorrow to collect the things."

With that he was off, humming a tune as he walked, waving to acquaintances through the camp as he went.

Mary sat quietly for a long time, angry at herself. She thought: *I told him too much; that mind of his is going to be turning over the information I gave him. He's smart as a whip, crafty, and always thinking; there's a good chance that he will work out that it is Grenough who's offering to help me.* She felt like kicking herself. *I'm near seventeen, old enough to control my tongue and not blurt out things when I get excited by what someone else has said.*

After staring into the fire for a few more minutes, Mary shrugged and told herself that it was useless to fret over words already spoken. Then she sighed, stood up and went to retrieve her sewing kit.

CHAPTER FOUR
On the Muskingum

On the night of the fourth the army camped a few miles short of the remains of the old, long abandoned Indian village of Logstown, located on the shores of the Ohio. The next day they passed through the deserted village; the buildings were decrepit and falling down, for the place had been uninhabited since the early years of the French War. That night the army camped not far from the mouth of the Big Beaver. The next day they turned north and marched along the Beaver for several miles and forded at a shallow spot well to the north of the mouth; the bottom was covered with stones which made wading tricky. Mary and Kathryn lifted their skirts in an effort to stay as dry as possible and then gritted their teeth at the shock of the cold water. Kathryn promptly tripped over a stone; Mary tried to place her feet carefully but eventually stepped into a hole in the river bed. Both ended up with soaked clothing. They spent most of the day's march shivering, teeth chattering in the cold air as their garments slowly dried. Progress crossing the stream was hampered greatly by the recalcitrance of the bullocks and sheep.

Enroute to the ford, the column passed a recently abandoned village. It was quite small and Mary could see that the residents had left in great haste; the log and bark lodges were intact and abandoned possessions lay about between structures. Some chickens pecked at the ground. After the crossing, they turned northwesterly and soon came across another hastily abandoned village.

Late in the morning, Mary, walking beside Kathryn and the two male orderlies, looked up to see Baird standing ahead of her, holding his tall bay by the reins and letting the column flow around him. Then he saw Mary; a great smile came over his face and he waved at her. "Hello, Mary! How's my favorite Highland lass?"

"Joshua! What are you doing back here with the column?"

Baird walked beside her, the horse trailing behind. "I came back in to brief Bouquet about the lay of things ahead."

"And what does that happen to be? Everyone's tense here in the column, wondering what the Indians are going to do." She motioned back toward the last village. "I've already seen two empty villages, Joshua."

"And you'll see a lot more. We've got a good bunch of scouts workin' for the army: Alex Lowrey, Andy Boggs, Sam Brown, and Tom Mitchell. I've known most of them for a good while. Those boys know their business. They're ranging in a wide path well ahead of the army. We've all picked up the trails of many bands as they retreat westward. There be little doubt the Indians are falling back toward the Muskingum. There's a concentration of large villages, particularly Delaware and Mingo, along that river."

Mary asked, "Why do you think they are doing that? Doc Munro is worried they may be pulling back to gather their warriors."

Joshua shrugged. "That could be; perchance the chiefs have already decided to fight and they want to collect their women and children and old ones beyond the Muskingum for protection, so they can be free to attack us in the territory between the Beaver and that river."

Mary's brow furrowed. "They could be pretty powerful if they can combine all their strength, like at Braddock's battle and Bushy Run last year. How many would we have to fight?"

"If all the tribes get together, I figure we'd face 800 to 1,000." He looked down at her. "That's nearly as many soldiers as we got, and if they do put their people across the Muskingum, they'll be free to run wild around us while we got to protect the baggage and supplies."

Mary nodded. "Just like it was at Bushy Run; the Indians could move through the forest and attack from every side; we had to protect the packhorses carrying supplies for Pitt."

"Yeah, that's right enough." Joshua agreed. He looked into the distance, lost in thought. Then he said, "There's somethin' else that might be on the minds of the sachems and war captains: Getting enough ammunition. We ain't got no idea how much powder and lead they actually have. If they're in short supply, they can't fight, 'cause they'll need what they got for the long winter hunt. And they used a lot of ammunition during the raids in '63, the battle at Bushy Run, and then the raiding earlier this year."

"But you said — back at Pitt — there was a ring of men providing them with munitions. Maybe they've been at work and the tribes have what they need."

"Could be, Mary." Then Baird grinned. "Of course, Wend stopped a powerful big load of powder and lead when he killed those men up in the mountains north of Fort Littleton back in June. He blew it all to hell and gone. That was a load which would have supplied many war parties."

They walked in silence for a moment.

Then Joshua continued, "But it's still a puzzle to me." He paused and then said, "Fact is, the hostiles know exactly where we are. There are scoutin' parties of Delawares, Mingoes, and Shawnees all around us; just watchin'. I see sign of them all the time, and have caught glimpses of warriors once and a while."

"But what you're saying is that it could be we'll not know whether the Indians will fight until we get to the Muskingum River?"

Joshua nodded, a thoughtful look on his face. "Mary, it might be longer than that. It could be we ain't goin to know the answer 'till we get to the next river to the west of the Muskingum — the Scioto."

"God, Joshua. It seems this country is just one river after another. The river we crossed this morning was nearly the death of me. I'm still shivering. But why is the Scioto so important?"

"There be a passel of big Shawnee villages along that stream; the towns of important chiefs and sachems. Their most powerful chief is named Cornstalk. And the Shawnee — well, we always thought they be the tribe which is most likely to be for war." Joshua shrugged his shoulders. "But afore we left, Bouquet got word from some of his Indian friends in the Ohio Country. There's a heated argument goin' on among the Shawnee sachems; it seems at least some of them are ready for peace. But those who want war are led by a hothead named Charlot Kaske. He's a half-caste; his father was German and his mother was Shawnee. And he's married to a white woman who was taken hostage years ago."

"I don't understand, Joshua. How did such a man become so set against the whites?"

"Yeah, well, I seen this before in the Indian world; sometimes white hostages or men and women of mixed heritage become more Indian than the Indians themselves. I've thought on it a lot; seems to me they feel they must prove themselves." He thought a moment, then looked at Mary. "Now you take that Abigail; Wend Eckert offered her a way back to the English world and she turned him flat down. Said she loved him, but she vowed her place was with the Mingo. And that even though her bein' with a child by Wend."

"What? Wend had a child with Abigail Gibson?" Mary was shocked. She walked in silence for a moment, then shook her head and said slowly and quietly, almost to herself, "I had no idea."

"It's true: a little boy with brown hair and blue eyes; he be about five years old by now. Wend himself didn't know nothin' about it until we found Abigail in that village on Slippery Rock Creek."

They walked is silence for a while longer. Then Joshua said, "I met this Kaske once; he's a big fellow, takes after his father. But he's a great warrior and a big orator at the counsel fires. That kind of man can attract a lot of young braves who are lookin' to make a name for themselves in war. And chiefs who want to keep their power have to go along if they want their young warriors to stay loyal."

* * *

As October wore on, the expedition pushed on through a forest of increasingly colorful foliage. The advance was ponderous, rarely making more than eight to ten miles good per day as the axe men laboriously cut three parallel trails. Mary Fraser imagined that from a bird's eye view, the advance must look like the path of three giant moles burrowing along the earth in parallel. In fact, the days began to merge into sameness, each becoming a near copy of the last, the grinding march broken only by the need to cross streams or navigate ridges.

Munro, repeating conversations at the officer's mess, told the hospital staff that Bouquet was quite satisfied with the pace, for he wanted the Indians to develop the sense that their advance was inexorable, and realizing that, understand that there was no option except to treat for peace.

Mary spent evenings focused on her lessons. Mostly she worked alone by the fire or by the light of a lantern in the hospital area, but sometimes she spent time with Chaplain MacLagen. It was because of one of those sessions that she was able to have elements of the strategic plan of the campaign explained to her.

As they sat before his tent, the chaplain said, "All right, once again, count to ten, Mary."

Mary concentrated to remember the strange words. "Un, deux, trois, quatre, cinq, six, sept, huit, neuf, dix."

MacLagen nodded and answered in French. "Bon, Marie! Well, you have that down. Now let's learn from eleven to twenty."

Suddenly a male voice said, "Learning French; now that's a new challenge for Miss Fraser."

Mary looked around and saw Captain Charles McDonald and another officer standing a few feet from the chaplain's tent. They had obviously been listening for a while. She stood up, made a small curtsy, and said, "Bonsoir, mon Capitaine."

McDonald threw his head back and laughed. "Very good, Miss Fraser. You've obviously been applying yourself." He looked at the chaplain. "Why the lessons in the language of our esteemed former enemy?"

MacGlagen said, "Miss Fraser is studying to become a governess, Charles. It is my experience that most families want their children to learn French, the language of diplomacy, romance, and poetry. Knowledge of the language is something of a prerequisite for a governess or children's tutor."

McDonald cocked his head reflectively for a moment. "Never thought of it, but damned if I don't think you're right, Chaplain. Capital idea for Miss Fraser and I know she"ll be good at it."

Mary said, "Thank you, Captain McDonald." Then she turned to the other man, who wore the uniform of an Ensign in the Royal Americans. "Sir, weren't you the engineer at Fort Pitt in 1759? You look like the man who I watched lay out the fort. My family was with Captain James Robertson's company that winter."

McDonald said, "This is Ensign Thomas Hutchins, Mary. He is the engineer of this expedition."

Hutchins touched his cap to Mary, then said, "Yes, I was at the forks of the Ohio under the garrison commander, Captain Mercer. And I was very glad to have Robertson there to help me; James is an excellent engineer. He and his men of the 77th did a lot of the preliminary work on the fort."

Mary said, "Yes, I know. I used to watch all the time."

Hutchins froze and stared at Mary for a moment. Then a broad smile broke over his face. "By God, I know you! You're that little red haired girl who used to stand by watching our work every day!"

"Yes, Mr. Hutchins, there wasn't much else to do for a child that winter."

The ensign looked over Mary appraisingly. "Well, miss, you're certainly all grown up now!"

Then Mary said, "But back then, sir, you were a lieutenant wearing the green coat of the Pennsylvania Regiment."

"Yes, quite correct. But I obtained an Ensign's commission in the 60th soon after that."

McDonald put his hand on Hutchin's shoulder. "Mr. Hutchins is like the navigator on a ship. He plots our course through the wilderness and shows Bouquet where we are. He goes out with the scouts all the time to pick the best land for us to cut the road."

Hutchins said, "Yes, and I just arrived back in camp this afternoon. I was out with scouts to lay out our way to the North Branch of the Muskingum —in fact, we're almost there."

Mary smiled. "Sir, it must be very interesting. I remember watching you working with your instruments at Pitt, but of course, I never knew what they were called and what they did."

Hutchins smiled. "Well, McDonald and I are on our way to my tent now. Why don't you come along and I'll show you the map of our progress and my instruments." He turned to MacLagen and asked, "That is, if it's all right with your tutor?"

MacLagen grinned broadly. "Of course; it would be most educational. Mary and I can get back to French tomorrow."

It was actually only a short distance to Hutchin's tent, which was part of Bouquet's headquarters complex. Under the fly was an improvised table with a paper affixed to the surface. The engineer motioned both of his visitors to join him at the table. Hutchins pointed to the paper on the surface, which contained a rough map. He said, "This is the field sketch of our progress to date." He traced out a line which had been plotted on the map. "This is our track. We started at the Allegheny, across from Pitt, then we moved along the Ohio down to Logstown, turned northwest and crossed the Beaver and continued northwest until we got near the Great Trail, which runs roughly east-west through the Ohio Country. We traveled westward near the Great Trail for several days, then turned southwest to approach the North Branch of the Muskingum, or as the Indians call it, the Tuscarawas River." He put his finger on the end of the line. "That's where we are now, about a day's march from the river. We've marched roughly a 100 miles since we left our first camp."

McDonald turned to Mary. "Ensign Hutchins spends a great deal of time out with the scouts, marking our planned path and locating suitable campsites." He grinned at her. "It's accurate to say that where we go, he's been."

"That could be quite dangerous, Mr. Hutchins," Mary responded.

Hutchins shrugged. "Well, there's always at least one scout with me and a detachment of the light horse. And so far we've not had any interference from war parties."

McDonald said, "And the fact is, Ensign Hutchins is nearly as familiar with this country as any of the scouts. He's traveled all the way up to the lakes and then down through the Muskingum country and many of the villages along it."

"After I left the Pennsylvania Regiment, I worked for Sir William Johnson as an Indian agent for a while. Then, when I received my British Army commission, I was sent on an exploratory mission to chart the lake country and the Ohio area for the Crown. It was during the relative peace with the Indians in '61-62. I made a circuit from Pitt up to Detroit, then through this very territory, making maps as I went." He smiled at Mary. "Of course, I was accompanied by some rough men who knew the country."

Mary was impressed. "But even so, Mr. Hutchins, it was a daring trip." She thought a moment, and said, "And fortunate for us that you were able to gain such knowledge of the country."

"I flatter myself that it has been of some use to Colonel Bouquet."

Mary said, "Can I ask where we will be going in the next few days?"

Hutchins smiled. "Of course, Miss Fraser," He ran his finger along the map. "We go into camp very close to the Muskingum tomorrow and cross the river itself the next day. Then, if things go as planned, we follow the river south toward the main concentration of Delaware and Mingo villages."

Mary thought for a second and then remembered what Joshua had told her. She studied the map for a second. "So in a few days at the outside, the Indians will have to make a decision to either fight or begin negotiations."

"Yes, Miss Fraser, that is quite correct, and as a matter of fact, it is the Colonel's intent to drive them to that decision."

Mary looked at Hutchins. Then she moved her finger to the Scioto and continued, "Or they could abandon their villages and flee west to join the Shawnee and make a fight with combined forces like we faced at Bushy Run."

McDonald and Hutchins looked at each other, surprise in their faces. McDonald said, "That's all very perceptive, Miss Fraser."

"Yes," said Hutchins, "You've just touched on the major question of the campaign. And no one has the answer."

Mary felt proud of herself at being able to show her knowledge. She looked back down at the sketch map. "Mr. Hutchins, how are you able to plot our position so precisely?"

Hutchins' face lit up. "I'm glad you asked that question, Miss Fraser. It gives me a chance to show you my instruments." He turned and picked up a compass. "This is a military field compass, one of the most basic of instruments. As you can see, it has a pair of sights almost like a rifle, so you can mark the direction to a certain point precisely."

Mary had seen compasses before, but none so elaborate. But the instrument which attracted her keenest attention was mounted on a tripod. She pointed and asked, "Is that a compass also?"

Hutchins went over to the tripod and waved for Mary to join him. "This is called a *circumferentor*. It is a more complex form of compass, marked in 360 degrees. Like the compass, it has sights, and the device can be rotated. It's used to measure precise angles in the horizontal plane."

Mary examined the device and then nodded her understanding to Hutchins.

"Now, for distance, we use these." Hutchins opened one of the chests. "These are called Gunter's chains. Each one has 100 links of precise length, and each chain is precisely sixty-six feet long. That's the standard length in the surveying profession."

Mary was about to ask why the chains were such an odd length, instead of an even length like 100 feet, when Lieutenant Faulkner of the 60th, who had replaced Welford as Bouquet's adjutant, arrived. He cleared his throat and said, "Thomas, the colonel needs to see you at his tent at your earliest convenience, which in this case means you're to come back with me now."

"What's afoot Faulkner?" Hutchins asked. He winked at McDonald and Mary. "Are the tribes mustering to attack?"

"Precisely the opposite, Thomas. The scout Baird has just ridden into camp. While ranging to the northwest, he encountered two couriers bringing dispatches from Colonel Bradstreet in Detroit and brought them along with him. However, the dispatches are not the important thing. The couriers were captured by the Delaware just a few miles from here. But when the Delaware chiefs found out they were on their way to see Bouquet, they released them and gave them a message for the colonel."

Faulkner looked at all three of them and grinned.

McDonald exclaimed, "Don't just stand there grinning like an idiot jester, Faulkner. Tell us what you know!"

"The message is that a large number of Indian chiefs are coming in to negotiate peace. They're gathering now and will proceed to a point we designate in a few days. That's why Bouquet want's you, Hutchins; you're to help select a good site for the meeting."

Hutchins quickly asked, "Are the Shawnee chiefs coming in?"

"The message is just from the Delawares and Mingoes. There's no word from the Shawnees."

McDonald said, "Damn! I fear the Shawnee will be obstinate. And we're running out of good weather."

Hutchins shook his head. "There'll be the devil to pay if we can't finish this campaign in the next few weeks. And God knows what the political implications will be if we have to come back next year to deal with the Shawnee."

McDonald nodded. "By God, you're right; there'll be outrage in Philadelphia and Gage's headquarters at New York if the campaign can't be finished until next year."

Hutchins said, "Yes, Charles; and think of the expense." Then he turned to Mary. "I'm afraid we must break off our surveying lesson, Miss Fraser. But it would be my pleasure to resume when the press of events allows us." He grinned, "In the meantime, I'm afraid your French lessons will have to satisfy your desire for knowledge."

Hutchins picked up his hat and then the three officers strode off toward Bouquet's tent.

*   *   *

Three days later, on October 17th, Mary and Kathryn stood with Joshua Baird and Ensign Thomas Hutchins watching the first meeting of Colonel Bouquet and the Indian emissaries. The colonel and Indian chiefs were gathered in a "bower," a three sided shelter built from young trees and covered with canvas. Bouquet sat on a camp chair within the structure and was accompanied by Richard Grenough — who stood beside him — and an interpreter. The adjutant, Faulkner, also stood close at hand to assist as necessary. Paraded some distance in front of the bower was a formation of troops, the largest body being the grenadier companies of both the 42nd and 60th.

A council fire had been built directly in front of the bower and the chiefs sat on the ground on the other side of it from Bouquet.

Members of Bouquet's headquarters and the hospital staff were gathered at one side of the bower. On the opposite side were a small group of warriors and with them were a number of white hostages, which the Indians had brought with them. Mary counted eighteen of the Europeans.

Hutchins had a piece of paper clipped to a board and was making a sketch of the proceedings.

Mary turned to Joshua. "Why didn't the colonel arrange for chairs for the chiefs?"

Baird smiled wolfishly. "Bouquet had that all planned out. He made sure he's sitting higher than them; it shows he's the big man with the power and they're like the children sitting at the feet of the father."

Mary looked at the chiefs, their faces impassive. One held a string of wampum. "Who's the one with the wampum, Joshua?"

That's ole' Gayasuta himself, lass. I've seen him many a' time. He's a Mingo and has been the main organizer behind the insurrection here in the Ohio Country. I 'spect you'll hear him doin' most of the talkin' on the Indian side today."

Hutchins paused in his drawing for a moment. "Probably the second biggest chief here is Turtle's Heart, the Delaware. He played a large role in the siege of Fort Pitt last year. That's him next to Guyasuta."

"There are a lot of others there," Mary said. "Who are they? Are they all chiefs?"

"Not all chiefs, but if they're here, they be important, one way or another." Joshua motioned toward the Indians. "See that one sittin' quiet-like behind Guyasuta?

Mary nodded. "Yes; the one looking around, just taking everything in?"

"Yeah, lass; that be ole' Neolin himself. He a spiritual man they call 'The Profit.' He worked with both Guyasuta and Pontiac himself to stir things up and make the rebellion into a holy war against the whites. Now if I know him, I'd wager he won't say nothin' today. But when they all go back to their camps to talk things over, he'll be right in the middle of it."

Hutchins said, "Look, Joshua, Killbuck's here too. I hear he's been bragging about his mighty exploits at Bushy Run."

"Yeah, I see him Thomas. He can lie all day long about how mighty he was, but truth be told he ran away with the rest of them when Major Campbell and his two companies hit them with bayonets on the flank."

Hutchins looked at the scout and smiled. "Yes, Joshua, and don't think they aren't remembering that day when they sit there and look up at Bouquet."

Mary asked, "Who are the others? Are any of them Shawnees?"

Joshua said, "There be two more important Delawares here: Custaloga and Tamaqua. But there is one Shawnee chief; that be Keissinautchta. He's the king of a few small villages here around the Muskingum. I figure he only had two choices: Join with the Delawares and Mingoes and treat for peace, or abandon his villages and flee to the Scioto to join with the other Shawnees. So, since he's here, I 'spect he and his people decided they didn't want to give up everything and run west."

Mary looked at Baird and then Hutchins. "But the fact is, we still don't know what the rest of the Shawnees will do."

Hutchins said, "You are quite correct, Miss Fraser. There's no way that Keissinautchta can speak for the whole Shawnee tribe. Clearly we're going to have to find a way to bring them to the table."

Mary sighed. "So even if this group of chiefs accepts peace terms, we'll have to continue the campaign."

Hutchins looked at Mary and shook his head. "Yes, but I fear we don't have enough time to get to the Scioto and confront the Shawnee before the harsh weather arrives." He looked at Bouquet. "Don't think that isn't weighing heavily on the colonel's mind."

There had been some preliminaries going on during their discussion. But then Guyasuta stood up and began talking. He went on at great length; Bouquet's translator passed what he said to the colonel and Grenough, but Mary couldn't hear. She turned to Joshua and asked, "What are they saying?"

Baird grinned and shrugged his shoulder. "He started with lots of ceremonial stuff, then told Bouquet who all was here. Now he's down to the meat of it. Frankly, it's all horse dung. He's sayin' that this whole war was just a misunderstanding. The tribal chiefs from the northwest tribes — the Ottawa's, the Chippewa's, the Miami's and others led by that devil Pontiac — got the young bucks all stirred up for war. Then these here chiefs couldn't control their own young men and things just got out of hand."

Mary was astonished. "My God, hundreds of people have been killed or taken prisoner, forts captured and the garrisons massacred, scores of farms torched, and thousands of settlers living as refugees in towns back east, and he says it was all just a misunderstanding? That some young hotheads got carried away? Does he really expect Bouquet to believe that?"

"Naw, like I said its just lies to save face. Hell, there be no doubt Guyasuta had as much to do with startin' this war as Pontiac." Joshua put his hand to his ear. "Now he's sayin' that they all seriously want peace. And to show their intentions are honorable, they brought along some hostages to give back. That's why all those white people are here."

Mary nodded. "Yes, and that's why Munro was told to have the hospital staff here. Colonel Bouquet was expecting some hostages would be turned over as a sign of good faith. We're supposed to examine them to make sure they're all fit enough to travel and then they're going to be immediately sent back to Fort Pitt under escort."

There was a lot more talk; some of the other Indians spoke. It went on for a couple of more hours. Finally, the chiefs were finished, and Bouquet stood up. He told them he had listened to their stories and would consider what they had said. Moreover, he would give them his decision and his conditions for peace on the morrow.

Mary turned to Joshua. "Why wait until tomorrow? Hasn't he long ago decided what he wants from them?"

Joshua laughed. "Of course he has, lass. But he's following Indian custom. He has to wait a while to show them that he's seriously considering what they said today. It's a matter of appearances."

Hutchins nodded. "Joshua's right. We knew this would take at least two days. Bouquet's going to tell them tomorrow that they must stop hostilities, turn over all white prisoners they have, provide him with high ranking Indian hostages to show good faith, and then come to a more formal meeting next year to work out the final treaty."

Mary looked back at the bower to see that the Indians had risen and were leaving. A detachment of soldiers had formed around the white hostages to escort them to the hospital area.

Munro motioned to his staff. "Let's go see the hostages and then walk with them back to the hospital. We have a lot of work to do."

* * *

The hospital staff spent the rest of the day dealing with the hostages, all of whom were found to be in good shape and physically able to travel. However, as they worked, Mary became aware of a rapid change in the weather. A stiff wind from the northwest came up, bringing in dense cloud cover and frigid temperatures. Then, early in the night, a fierce storm broke over the Muskingum, sheets of rain pummeling the camp. Everyone in the military camp hunkered down in their tents, shivering and becoming soaked from leaks and flooding. Some tents were collapsed by the fierceness of the wind, the occupants forced to re-raise them in the midst of the mud and darkness or seek shelter elsewhere.

The storm persisted for the next two days. So it was not until the 20th that the council with the Indians could resume. The hospital staff were not at that meeting, which only lasted through the morning. But early in the afternoon, Munro came back from the officer's mess and told them about the results. The staff were sitting on logs around the fire drying out; the sun had finally appeared and the temperature moderated somewhat. But their shoes were in the deep mud which had resulted from the days of rain.

Munro looked over them and smiled as he talked. "Lieutenant Faulkner told me it was a short meeting. The colonel had his demands all listed on a piece of paper and essentially delivered an ultimatum to the chiefs. And then he told them that they had until the first day of next month — twelve days from now — to deliver up their white prisoners. Then he admonished them that if they didn't comply, he would have no choice but to initiate hostilities." He paused and grinned broadly. "Apparently they took his words to heart, for they made haste to depart for their villages, saying they would need every minute of the time to gather up the hostages."

Shortly the staff went back to work, and it was only about a half hour later that Mary saw Baird standing by the hospital fire, holding the reins to his hunter,

Beau. The horse was fitted with a bedroll and saddlebags. Joshua motioned for her to come see him.

Mary said, "It looks like you're going out on a scout, Joshua. Are you to check that the Indians are doing what they promised?"

"Bouquet's sending out others to do that. Me and Hutchins is going out to scout our route over the next few days and find good campsites."

Mary was puzzled. "You mean we're not staying at this camp? Won't the Indians expect us to be here so they can deliver their hostages?"

Joshua laughed. "Naw, Bouquet is figuring to get into the chief's minds. We're going to continue south, right down to the biggest concentration of villages here along the Muskingum. That'll keep the Indians on edge, cause they'll know we're in a positon to attack easily if they don't live up to our demands. Henry used a big word to describe what he was doin'," Joshua bit his tongue and looked up to the sky a moment to think. "I think he called it 'intimidation.' Yeah, that was the word." He looked at Mary. "Would that be a word that means puttin' the pressure on the tribes?"

Mary laughed and nodded. "It would indeed, Joshua."

"Yeah, well then, we're gonna' move south an' intimidate the chiefs." He waved around. "So you better get ready to move; Bouquet says he plans to march tomorrow. Three good days and we'll be down at Wakatomika. That's the name of the place where several villages are. We'll wait there for the Indians to bring in their prisoners."

Mary looked around. "Moving would be a good idea. At least that will get us out of all this deep mud we've stirred up after the rain. I don't believe I'm ever going to get my shoes clean again."

As Joshua had indicated, the army spent the next three days again on the advance, this time moving relentlessly southward along the Muskingum. Then they halted and built a more extensive camp than had been the norm during the long march out from Fort Pitt. Shelters, called "Houses of Ease" were constructed over the latrines. The troops built more substantial barricades at their positions on the perimeter of the camp. A new, larger bower was assembled for the continuation of negotiations with the tribal leaders. Finally, the engineers laid out a place near the bower where cabins would be built to house the hundreds of prisoners which would be received if the tribes in fact complied with Bouquet's ultimatum to turn over white prisoners.

And as the days progressed, it became clear that the Delawares and Mingoes were planning to comply. Obviously the chiefs had sent runners to villages all over the Ohio Country. Soon an Indian camp began to spring up alongside the military position as numerous tribal bands, including warriors, women, and children began to arrive. The expedition's scouts ranged the forestland and watched the progress of the Indian parties, noting that some of them were coming from great distances, and the keen eyes of the scouts could pick out numerous white faces among the travelers.

A spirit of optimism spread through the camp in the hope that the campaign was nearing its end. But the unspoken question on everyone's mind was: What of the Shawnee?

CHAPTER FIVE
Consequential Encounters

J ust after morning rounds had been completed, Mary Fraser gathered up discarded dressings and bandages in her arms and walked along the row of tents toward the kettle where they boiled the bandages. The two surgeons had left to report in to the headquarters of their respective regiments, and the two medical orderlies had also departed on various errands. Mary and Kathryn were alone with the patients in the hospital.

Mary looked up and then suddenly stopped, startled at what she saw. Standing at the edge of the bush just beyond the hospital tents stood a tall woman in Indian clothing. The woman looked to be in her early twenties and she had long blond hair pulled back into a single braid which hung down her back. A plain, undyed linen shift, belted at the waist was her main article of clothing, and she wore a blanket coat for protection against the fall chill. A pair of soft, beaded moccasins were on her feet. Perhaps the most startling thing about the woman was her blue, piercing eyes which gave her a look of great concentration and dignity. Nearly as startling was the appearance of the little boy who stood beside her; Mary guessed he was about five years old. He was tall for his age and had brown hair and blue eyes and wore a coat of the same material as the woman.

Instantly, Mary knew she was looking at Abigail Gibson and Wend Eckert's son. She stood silent for a moment, dealing with the shock of the encounter.

Meanwhile, Abigail took the boy's hand and advanced until she was in front of Mary. She stood there, appraising the nurse for a moment, the blue eyes seeming to drill into Mary, and then said quietly, "My name is Orenda. I'm with the Mingo of Slippery Rock Creek."

Mary said quickly, "You're not supposed to be here. The people of the tribes are required to stay in their camp areas." Then another thought occurred to her. "How did you get here through the camp guards and the sentinels?"

Abigail shrugged. "I've been living with the Mingo for five years; moving through the forest without being seen or heard is something I learned long ago." She smiled. "I've been watching since early this morning from the trees. I saw the doctors and other men leave. I know that you are alone here with just one other woman."

A twinge of fear coursed through Mary. Were there other Indians out in the bush watching them? Her eyes inadvertently shifted to the forest beyond the other woman.

Abigail made a thin smile as she caught Mary's eye movement and understood the meaning. She shook her head. "No, there's no danger. I'm here alone with just my son." She paused and tentatively reached out and touched Mary's arm. "I'm here to ask a favor, one woman to another."

Mary almost burst out with the woman's real name and that she knew her story. But then she realized she would have to explain her relationship with Wend and that might complicate her dealings with this woman. So she restrained the impulse and instead simply said, "A favor? What kind of favor. Then she looked down at the boy and said, "Is your son sick?"

Abigail looked down at the child, squeezed his hand and smiled. The little boy looked up at her and smiled back. In an instant Mary's heart skipped a beat, for the twinkle in his eyes and the grin on his face was an exact duplicate of Wend's.

"No, he's fine. The favor is for my people."

"Then I'm not sure what you mean."

"I act as the doctor for my village and all the other villages in our valley. I learned medicine before I was captured." Abigail's face turned reflective and she stared off into the distance for a moment. Then she sighed and said softly, "That was five years ago on Forbes Road; just at the base of Sideling Hill."

Mary forced a stern look on her face. "That's interesting. But please explain what you want from me."

"I'm worried about the smallpox. There have been epidemics running through the Ohio Country. Right now it's not as bad as it was a couple of years ago, but I'm worried that it might come back next year. The more contact we have with white people, the more severe the outbreak. My village is so small, an outbreak could devastate us. It might wipe us out."

Mary shrugged her shoulders. "But what can I do to help that?"

"A little before I was captured, I read about a way to expose people to a small amount of the contagion so that they became immune." She thought a moment, her face wrinkled up in concentration. "The word that was used was *inoculation,* I think."

Mary nodded. "Yes, yes, that is the word. You take some of the fluid from the sore of a person who has the disease and put it into the blood of a person who is unaffected. And then they can't get the disease, or at least not as bad as before."

Abigail smiled. "Yes, that's what I heard about. But the article I was reading didn't have the details of how it was done. I want to be able to do it for my village; but I realize that if I don't do it exactly the right way, the result could be disastrous. Do you know how it's done? Can you instruct me?"

Mary thought for a moment. "But you don't need to know that. If a treaty is signed, the Mingoes will be required to turn you over to us. Your days with the savages will be over."

A stern look came over the other woman's face. "The *Mingo* are *not* savages and they are my people now. And I want to stay with them. My husband, Wolf Claw, and the elders of my village will never let me be turned over. They'll hide me. And the same will happen with many other captives who feel the same way. The British are dreaming if they think all of the hostages will be sent home."

Mary shook her head. "But that's the policy. And besides, I can't help you. I'm just a nurse."

"Isn't there a book in the hospital? I can read; I can read very well. That's how I learned my medicine. There must be a book that explains how to do these inoculations."

"I can't let you look at the doctor's books. I'd get in trouble."

"I beg you; just give me a few minutes with a book which explains the procedure. I have a good memory. That's all that I'll need."

Mary looked at the woman and then at the little boy, the tiny version of Wend, and made up her mind. "Come with me," she said, and led them to the treatment tent. "Stay here a moment."

Walking briskly to Munro's tent, she grabbed the new medical reference and took it back to where Abigail waited. She put the book down on the table under the tent fly and quickly opened it to the section on smallpox. "You'll find what you are looking for here. I read it myself just a few days ago."

Abigail smiled warmly at Mary and then leaned over to start reading. Mary noted that her mouth moved as she worked deciphering the text.

She paused and looked up again at Mary, embarrassment in her face. "It's been five years since I did much reading. Some of the words come hard."

Mary was about to answer when suddenly a loud, angry sounding male voice interrupted them.

"Mary Fraser, what the devil is going on here?"

Mary looked up to see Surgeon Munro standing in front of the tent; Highsmith stood behind him. Mary bit her lip, trying to think what to say.

Munro said, "Just don't stand there, Miss Fraser. Explain what this person is doing."

Abigail snapped the book shut and took hold of her son's hand.

Mary finally found words. "This woman is with the Mingoes. She wanted some medical information. I was going to let her read what the reference book says."

Munro's face was turning red. He addressed himself to Abigail. "The people from the tribes are not allowed within the military lines. You must return to your own camp. We cannot provide the assistance which you request."

Abigail stood up, a grim look on her face. She made a small curtsy to Munro and then she spoke, in the precise English of an educated lady, "Well Doctor, I had supposed that a man of medicine would be interested in helping his fellow humans as much as possible." She smiled thinly. "I see that is not the case for surgeons in the British Army. Pray forgive me for my mistake."

Munro was momentarily taken aback by her dignity and proper English. But he quickly recovered and retorted, "I have my orders. And they specify that there is to be no interchange with the tribal people until a treaty has been negotiated. I expect that you and your son will be very welcome, and we will provide every treatment possible, when that is done. Until then you must return to your lines." He motioned toward the bush.

Abigail stared at the surgeon for a long moment, her piercing eyes drilling into his, the suppressed anger clearly evident. Then she turned to Mary, gave her a simple nod, and leading the boy, left the tent and walked back toward the tree line. In a few moments the pair disappeared into the forest.

Munro turned on Mary. "Miss Fraser, I am nearly speechless. You knew the orders as well as I. What could you have been thinking?"

"I simply wanted to help her."

"You could not possibly have misunderstood Colonel Bouquet's orders that I read to everyone in the hospital the day we arrived in this camp. They expressly prohibit contact with the enemy by anyone except members of the negotiating party." He paused a moment, then said, "Do you realize that you could be lashed for what you have done?" He shook his head. "I've seen it done, even to women, for much less of a transgression."

Mary answered slowly. "I'm sorry, Mr. Munro. The woman was very sincere and I thought there would be no harm."

Munro waved his hands in frustration. "I have extended you the courtesy of access to my private reference book for your education and this is how you pay me back. Do you understand what shame would attend to the hospital if word of this got out within the regiment?"

Mary hung her head. But inside, she was encouraged by the surgeon's words, for they clearly indicated that he was not going to report her. "Yes, Mr. Munro."

"And I might point out that if you were punished, it could undo all your hopes for the future. Why just this day, Mr. Grenough spoke to me and the Chaplain. He asked for your full name and age, and the details of your education and experience as a nurse, so that he could prepare a letter of recommendation for you in your quest for household service." He shook his head. "That could all go by the board if your record showed punishment for your actions here."

For the first time Mary felt real fear. The thought of losing the influential merchant's letter devastated her. "I'm terribly sorry, sir. I guess I didn't think things out clearly."

"No, I daresay you didn't. This is not like you at all. Now, I'll not have you punished officially, Mary. But I do have the reputation of the hospital to think of. I must do something to help you perceive the seriousness of your act."

"Yes, doctor, I understand."

Munro raised a finger. "Here's my decision." He pointed toward the table. "I'm rescinding your privilege of reading that book, at least for the present. You're on probation, Miss Fraser. Your behavior in the future will determine if your access will be restored. And any further indiscretions will be reported to the commandant of the regiment. Do we understand each other?"

"Yes, doctor. I promise that you'll have no reason to regret your decision."

Munro nodded, "See that you keep that promise." Then he picked up the book and returned to his tent.

Doctor Highsmith stood watching Munro until he disappeared into the tent. Then he turned to Mary. His face was stern, but she could see a twinkle in his eyes. "You know, Mary, speaking personally, I might just have let that woman read the medical reference." He broke into a smile. "But then, the British are always saying that we provincials just don't have the same level of discipline as the regulars. I don't know but what that's true."

"I *have* heard that said, sir."

"Yes, it's a damn shame; we're rather incorrigible here in the colonies."

Mary smothered the urge to laugh outright. "Indeed, that's true, sir."

Highsmith shook his head. "But be that as it may, Mary, it happens that I have my own copy of the same reference volume as Surgeon Munro." He looked conspiratorially at her. "Now I've observed that Percy spends most of his evenings over at the mess with the other officers of the 42nd. If you don't mind reading by candlelight, you can look at my book in the women's tent when he doesn't happen to be around." He grinned broadly. "I assume you can maintain confidentiality about this arrangement?"

"Oh yes, sir! You can trust my discretion, sir."

"Good. I'll leave the book in plain view in my tent. You can come take it when you have time to read and old Munro has gone over to consume spirits and trade lies with his brother officers."

With that, Highsmith winked at her and then turned and strode out of the hospital toward the camp of the Pennsylvanians, walking with a seaman's rolling gait.

* * *

Late the next afternoon, Richard Grenough sat at the treatment table while Mary unwrapped the bandage from his right hand and removed the dressing. Mary made pleasant conversation while she worked. As she finished, Munro arrived to examine the splinter wound in the merchant's hand and Mary stood by observing.

"Well, this seems to be healing nicely, Mr. Grenough," said the surgeon.

"Believe me, Percy, there's still pain when I move my fingers."

"Yes, and that will persist for a while. But from what I can see, you have full use of your hand, sir. There's quite a red scar, but that will fade in time." Munro paused and examined the hand some more, turning it back and forth and manipulating the fingers. "Truthfully, sir, we've done all we can here. From now on, it's just a matter of time."

Both men rose, and after some pleasantries, Munro left to attend to other patients.

Grenough stood by the table and looked over at Mary, a pleasant smile on his face. His eyes looked right into hers. "You know, Miss Fraser, I've been hearing some very impressive things about you from Chaplain MacLagen and Surgeon Munro. They tell me you're extremely bright and have, in a most studious manner, worked to improve yourself."

Mary felt a surge of embarrassment. She fumbled for words. "I, . .. I do try my best, sir. Sometimes it's very hard while we're on the march."

Grenough cocked his head. "Hard? I would say it takes exceptional perseverance and determination, young lady; very admirable traits indeed."

"Thank you, sir."

"Well, I'm the kind of man who thinks such perseverance should be rewarded. And I've learned from MacLagen that you want to enter the service of a family as a children's tutor or governess. Am I not correct?"

"Yes, that is my fondest desire, sir. I love children and would do anything to spend my life helping to nurture them and provide the education they need for their place in society." She paused and looked directly at the merchant. "But to be perfectly honest, Mr. Grenough, I would also like to make for myself a more comfortable and gracious life than the army can provide."

Grenough smiled like a benevolent father. "Now that was very well stated, Miss Fraser. And I might say, very practical. Let me assure you, there's nothing wrong with being ambitious." He paused and then said, "I have some time on my hands now that we're here in a camp for a few days and it seems like there's a pause until all the Indian tribes have come in. I should take great pleasure in using the time to write a letter of introduction for you which might help you obtain a position with a family of substance. Would you like that?"

"Oh my, sir! You would have my eternal gratitude and appreciation. You are very thoughtful, Mr. Grenough."

"MacLagen was correct. You keep your wits about you and are very well spoken. I shall apply myself to composing the letter and then will send word to you when it is complete. My tent is not far from headquarters; you can come over to pick up the letter and I'll talk with you about several families I know that might be able to use your services."

Mary gave Grenough her best smile. "That would be marvelous, Mr. Grenough. I'll be waiting for your summons. And thank you again, sir."

"Not at all, not at all, Miss Mary Fraser. I shall be seeing you very soon with an epistle which I think you will find most gratifying and ultimately very useful to you." Grenough put his hat back on his head, touched the brim to her, and then strode off through the camp in the direction of headquarters.

* * *

Grenough's summons came in the evening of the next day. Mary, as excited as she had ever been in her life, made her way in the gathering dusk through the camp toward the location of Grenough's tent site. She had put on the blue traveling gown which her mother had salvaged long ago from the wreckage of the Eckert-Gibson caravan after the massacre in 1759. It was worn, faded, and patched, but it was the best she had and the only piece of clothing which hadn't been made by either herself or her mother or salvaged from the belongings of dead camp followers. Moreover, having been Abigail's, it was of stylish design and tailored of expensive fabric, and she wanted the merchant to get some idea of what her appearance might be if she were actually working in a house of the gentry.

The camp was busy, but when she got to the area where most of the officers lived, it was nearly empty because Colonel Bouquet had called a meeting to brief them on plans for the negotiations and the return of white hostages. That had included Surgeons Munro and Highsmith, for they would have an important role in caring for the white returnees.

Grenough was lounging in a chair under the fly in front of his tent, a pewter cup in hand. A cheery fire crackled in front of the fly. He stood as Mary approached. "Ah! Miss Fraser! And right on time; I do appreciate punctuality."

"Well, I try, Mr. Grenough. I believe that would be one of the requisites for someone in service."

"Of course, of course; how very perceptive." The merchant looked Mary over. He waved his hand at her and bowed slightly. "Let me say, that is a lovely gown, Miss Fraser, and the color complements your complexion and auburn hair extremely well. The ability to dress appropriately is an attribute which any employer would value."

"Thank you, sir. I do try, even though it is sometimes hard in a military camp."

"Naturally, but you do very well. I've noticed that your appearance has always been tasteful and attractive, including that regimental outfit you wear when we're on the march." Grenough paused and smiled at her, then motioned her to a camp chair beside the fire and attentively helped her into the seat.

Mary felt a wave of nervousness sweep over her, simultaneously accompanied by a warm glow. She had never been treated with such consideration by a gentleman of Grenough's stature. She sat down in the chair Grenough had indicated.

Grenough went to a decanter containing an amber liquid and filled another pewter cup. He offered it to Mary. "Here, take some of this whiskey. It will fortify you against this evening chill."

Mary hesitated. "Perhaps I shouldn't, Mr. Grenough. I'm here to talk with you about possible employers and I should keep my wits about me so I can remember what you say."

"Oh, nonsense, Miss Fraser; you forget I've seen you handle a jug of spirits like a man. Surely a cup of fine imported whiskey won't degrade your faculties. And besides, I'll give you a list of the names and addresses of the people we talk about, so you need have no worry of forgetting."

Mary took the cup and was about to take a sip when Grenough stopped her with a hand motion.

"Wait, let's have a toast, young lady." He raised his cup and proposed, "To the beginning of a productive relationship between us."

Mary raised her own cup in response and then took a sip. The whiskey was the smoothest and most tasteful liquor she had ever had. But after her sip a puzzling and worrisome thought came to her. She asked, "I'm not sure I fully understand your toast, Mr. Grenough. You speak of mutual benefit; clearly your letter will benefit me, but I'm not sure how I can assist you. Is there something you desire from me?"

Grenough grinned broadly, cocked his head, and seemed to chuckle to himself. Then he took another sip of his drink and then said, "Indeed, you are a perceptive young lady." He paused for a moment as if carefully choosing his words. "Well, when you have proven yourself of great service to some family, they will remember that it was I who recommended you, and feel indebted. I always like to have people of influence indebted to me."

Mary nodded and said, "Now that I can understand, sir."

"Now let's talk about some of the families who might be interested in your services." Grenough began naming a series of well-to-do families who he said had young children. They ranged from wealthy merchants and lawyers living in large towns like Philadelphia and New York to planters in the Maryland and Virginia tidewater. He discussed their background and what he knew about their children and even in some cases pointed out those he thought might currently be in need of a tutor or governess.

Mary was impressed with Grenough's easy familiarity with the privileged. It brought home to her how influential the man was and how fortunate she was that he had taken her under his wing.

They talked for an extended time, and Grenough pressed a second cup of whiskey upon her. Mary felt she couldn't refuse, and at any rate, the liquor tasted so refined and mild that she figured another round could do no harm. Then Grenough, finished with discussing possible employers for Mary, began talking about himself, his company, and his early life as first a hunter, then as a trader on the border in the time prior to and during the French War. He told her about how he had built his merchant and trading company into one of the largest on the border and settlement area and then he had expanded into providing supplies and transportation to the army.

In the middle of his talk, he gave Mary another cup of whiskey. Again Mary felt she couldn't refuse, but managed to accept only about a half cup. She was beginning to wonder why Grenough, a man famous throughout Pennsylvania for his wealth and influence, felt it necessary to impress her with the story of his life.

Finally, Grenough stopped talking. He stood up and looked down at Mary. "Well, I seem to be running on here. I'm sure I'm boring you."

Mary shook her head. "Oh, no, Mr. Grenough; I find it all very fascinating."

"Well, at any rate, it's time we really got down to business." He turned and casually walked into his tent through the open flap and Mary could see him looking down at papers on a small writing table lit by a candle lantern. He motioned to her, "Come over and take a look at what I have for you."

Mary stood up. As she did so, she felt unsteady on her feet. She realized: *That liquor had more effect on me than I thought.* After a few seconds she became steadier and walked eagerly into the tent, anxious to see what Grenough had written. The two stood next to each other, looking down at the table.

"You can see," Grenough said, "That I've prepared both a letter of recommendation and an extensive list of people with whom you can make inquiries." He motioned over the two papers with his hand. "Why don't you peruse them?"

He stepped back and Mary eagerly began reading the letter. Then suddenly she realized it had become dark in the tent. Mary looked up to see that Grenough had dropped the flap so that the only light was from the candle lantern. Mary felt a rising sense of concern which heightened when Grenough stepped over and stood close beside her.

"Mr. Grenough, I don't understand; why did you shut that flap?"

The merchant sat down in the desk chair. Suddenly he reached up and pulled Mary down onto his lap and held her tight. "Mary, surely you understood that you would have to reciprocate in some way for that letter? You even asked what I might want from you when we toasted."

"For God's sake, Mr. Grenough, I'm not yet seventeen!"

"Come now don't play games; you're a daughter of the camp; undoubtedly experienced enough to know there's a price for everything. And you're old enough to understand a man's nature and to know that a woman with your beauty would be desirable to a man of any age." He looked at her with a knowing expression. "I dare guess you've had a man by now."

She started to protest, "Mr. Gren . . ."

But he cut her off by pulling her to him and stifling her words with a kiss directly on her mouth. Mary pushed back with all her strength until there was some distance between their faces. "I don't know what you think, but I'm not some easy woman who will do anything to get what she wants. Pray let go of me!"

"Damn! I do love a girl with spirit! It arouses me even more. Oh, my beautiful, lusty Mary, we can have a fine time." And with that Grenough moved his right hand down to her bosom, deftly released a hook, and slid his hand onto her left breast. "I must have you, Mary."

In a burst of rage, Mary gave a massive push with both hands and was able to pull free of him. She sprang back from the chair and in an instant Grenough was also on his feet. He had a crooked grin on his face.

The two stood a couple of feet apart, momentarily staring at each other. Then Grenough said, in a cajoling tone, "Mary, surely you've seen officers with young mistresses to satisfy their needs while on campaign. Forget being in service with a family; can't you see how a relationship of that type between us could benefit you, not just here, but for the long term? I'm no mere officer; I have the money to keep you in style and leisure after this expedition is over."

Then Grenough grinned even more and took a step toward her, his arms extended in an attempt to recapture her. But now Mary was ready for him. With her right hand she reached down through a slit in the side of her gown and found the handle of the small, narrow-bladed dagger which was strapped in a sheath to her right thigh. She whipped it out, raised it to her left shoulder, and then, with all her strength, swept it in a wide arc at Grenough.

She had meant only to force him to step back, so that she would have time to turn and dart out of the tent. But his forward motion carried him into the dagger's arc. And even though the merchant turned his head leftward in an attempt to avoid the blow, the blade sliced him deeply from below his right ear down to the corner of his mouth.

He stepped back, groaning and holding his hand over his cheek. Blood oozed out from between his fingers and dripped down his face and onto his shirt and coat. "You little bitch! You fucking bitch; you cut me!" His eyes were wide in surprise. "I'll have you flogged for this! You'll have stripes on your back for life."

Meanwhile Mary had switched the dagger to her left hand, and with her right reached into a pocket which she had sewn into the gown. She pulled out the tiny Spanish pistol her mother had carried and, cocking the hammer, pointed it directly at Grenough's head. "I'll not hesitate to shoot! This may be a small pistol, but it will finish you if I put a ball in your face!" Then she ordered, "Back up, Grenough!"

The merchant's eyes opened wide and he began to comply. When he had taken two small steps backward, she reached out to the desk and grabbed the letter.

"You stupid tart, that will do you no good now. Not after this!"

"It'll not get me a position, but as long as you know I have it, I doubt you'll go to anyone in authority to charge me. I'll have evidence of why I was here. Think about that, Mr. Grenough. Think hard."

And with that, she backed out through the tent flap, into the growing evening darkness.

Her heart pounding like a drum, Mary ran and hid behind a nearby tent, putting away her weapons as she went. She could hear Grenough bellowing for his servant. At first she feared pursuit, but then realized that the main thing on Grenough's mind would be his wound.

Suddenly she felt moisture running down her cheeks and realized she was weeping. She wiped her faced and told herself she must concentrate. *What to do next?* Then it came to her, more from emotion that rational thought: *I must see Joshua. He'll know what to do.*

Suddenly a woman's voice spoke through the evening dusk. "And what has got sweet little Miss Fraser, the regimental pet, so upset?"

Mary looked around in panic. Then she saw the buxom form of Laurie McPhie standing by a clothesline strung between two trees. She had an armful of dry clothing in her arms, which she had obviously just taken down from the line. The woman had a sly smile on her face.

Mary took a deep breath and tried to speak calmly. "Laurie, what makes you think I'm upset?"

Laurie laughed. "Well, just a wee bit ago I saw you sitting with Mr. Grenough under his fly, having a bit of the gentleman's whiskey. Smilin' at him and making a good old time of it, you was. But just now you come running out of his tent like the devil himself was after you. Now the light ain't too good, but I can see you wiping your eyes." Laurie smiled slyly. "I could be wrong, dearie, but it looks to me like things didn't go so well for you in there."

"Laurie, I don't know what you're talking about or what you thought you saw. And for once in your life keep your thoughts to yourself."

Mary turned to leave. From behind she heard Laurie laughing again and then the laundress called out, "If you be needin' any advice on how to please a swell gentleman, just stop by sometime and talk with me!"

Mary hunched her shoulders, determined not to be baited by the woman. With as much dignity and calm as she could muster, she started walking toward where she knew the camp of the scouts was located. It was not far and she was there in minutes. She saw six men sitting around a fire in the darkness, a jug on the ground in front of them. Then her heart skipped, for Baird was there, joking and laughing with the others.

Mary attempted to attract Joshua's attention. She waved, and finally he noticed her standing at the edge of the fire's light. He smiled and waved gaily at her.

She mouthed, "Joshua, I must see you!" Then she motioned for him to join her.

Baird looked at her closely and concern suddenly spread over his face. He put down the mug in his hand and stood up, quickly walking to her. He stopped and stared at Mary. "Lass, what's the matter? Your face is all red." He reached out and touched her cheek with a gentle hand. "You've been cryin'!"

"Joshua, please take me back to the hospital. I need your company."

The scout gave her his arm, and they started walking in silence. But her tears continued until they reached the hospital. Joshua didn't ask any questions as they walked. He helped her get seated on a log before the fire and then joined her.

Finally he could restrain himself no longer. "For God's sake, what's wrong, Mary?"

She turned to him. "Oh God, there's a real mess: Richard Grenough tried to have his way with me, Joshua. He got me into his tent and attacked me." She outlined the merchant's stratagem for getting her to his camp and then into the privacy of the tent. Then she explained what had occurred inside. She held up her hand. "Here's the letter I snatched from his table."

Baird glanced at the letter and then shook his head. "I wish you had mentioned this to me earlier, when he first started noticing you. This is what Grenough does. His whole life has been findin' out how to use people for his own ends." He sighed. "I've known the man for a long time. He's got a wife, children, and a fine house in York. But the fact is, he has a taste for the girls; he chases after young women, usually of the lowest class. Over the years he has figured out how to take advantage of them in a way they can't get back at him." He looked at Mary. "If I had known he was taking notice of you, I could have warned you."

Mary broke into a new round of tears. "He's not the first man who ever tried to have his way with me. I'm used to that. But I respected him so much; he's reckoned such a great man in the colony. He's a big friend of Colonel Bouquet. And so when he offered to help me find a position, I didn't even suspect his motives. I feel so naïve."

She shuddered and completely broke down in tears, her hands to her face. "And I had such high hopes. Now they've all vanished, like clouds broken up and blown away by a great wind. Since I was a little girl, people in the army have been telling me I'm a fool for trying to better myself; I've never believed them. Now I wonder if they weren't right all the time."

Joshua put his arm around her shoulders and put his hand on her arm. "No, Mary, the smart people in the regiment admire you for what you're doing. You keep your dreams."

They sat there for a few minutes, sharing the night and the silence. Then Joshua said, "We've got to tell the provost what happened. He'll deal with Grenough."

Mary jerked her head up. She wiped her tears. Then she said emphatically, "No, Joshua. We can't do that."

"For God's sake; why not?"

"Because I don't think anyone would believe us. After all, Grenough is a rich representative of the Governor. And I'm just a girl of the camp. Whose word are they going to take?"

"But you've got Grenough's letter."

"Joshua, I took that only to make Grenough think twice about making up some story about me. But it won't really do me any good." She pulled the letter out. "Look at this; he hadn't signed it yet. If I try to show it to the provost, he'll just say I wrote it up myself." She paused and then said, "And Grenough will counter with a story that he caught me stealing something from his tent and that he got injured trying to stop me. That would help him explain everything. He's friends with all the officers in the expedition. Who do you think they'd believe?"

Joshua sighed and nodded slowly. "Aye, I fear you may be right at that."

"And even if the provost believed me, there would always be questions about my reputation. People will ask what I was doing in his tent. There'd be a question about why we had a fight; plenty of people would figure I was his mistress and we had a lovers quarrel. I'd not likely get any recommendation from the colonel of the regiment or anyone else who knew about the story." She thought for a moment. "We must keep this quiet and hope that Grenough does the same; saying he was injured by accident. Maybe my having the letter will at least force him to do that."

Baird gritted his teeth. "Lass, you be thinking far ahead of me. For my part, my head was just full of rage 'bout what Grenough did to you and my not bein' able to have stopped it. And findin' some way of payin' him back for what he done. But damned if I don't think you're right about keepin' the whole thing quiet. In the end, he weren't able to have his way and you ain't really any worse off. And as long as word doesn't get out, there ain't no doubt 'bout your good reputation with the officers of the battalion."

They sat in silence for a while longer. But Mary noticed that Joshua was grinding his teeth. "What's the matter Joshua?"

"Oh, there's somethin' I got to do. I been puttin' it off, but things has come to a head. Anyway, I got to leave now. I hate to do it with you in this way."

"It's all right, now Joshua. I'll sit here for a while and then go to sleep. The truth is, I feel so very weary."

Joshua hugged her tight and then stood up. "I'll come see you tomorrow. But get word to me if Grenough tries anything."

Mary nodded. "Thank you for helping me Joshua. I don't know what I would have done without you. There's no one else I can confide in."

Despite what she had said, Mary lingered by the fire, her mind in turmoil over the evening's events. She feared that she was wrong and that Grenough might find some way to report her. She kept looking for the sight of the provost's men making their way through the camp toward her.

But in the end the only person who came out of the darkness was Surgeon Highsmith. He was carrying a physician's medical bag and walked right up to the fire. He put the bag down and then to Mary's surprise, sat down on the log beside her.

She said, "Good evening, Doctor."

"Good evening, Mary. How are you feeling?"

Mary put on a brave face. "I'm fine, Mr. Highsmith. Just sitting here enjoying the night."

"No, Mary Fraser, you're *not* fine. You are very upset and you have every right to be." He paused and, looking into the flames, said, "About an hour ago I was in the 2nd Pennsylvania mess. Grenough's man servant came up to me, all excited, and said that Richard Grenough had had an accident with his razor and needed a doctor right away. He said they came to me 'cause I was from the Pennsylvania regiment and was the appropriate one to treat him. He said it should be kept in the family. I told him to tell his boss that I would be there as fast as I could get my bag." Highsmith paused and looked at Mary. "On my way, I ran into Joshua Baird. He saw my medical bag and figured where I was going. Then he told me some of what happened to you. He swore me to secrecy. And then I went on to treat Grenough."

Mary felt a flash of anger. "He wasn't supposed to tell anyone. I want to keep it very quiet."

"I think you're right; never fear I'll keep your secret. But anyway, I had a duty to treat Grenough, even if he is a scoundrel."

She nodded wearily, "Yes, I understand, Mr. Highsmith."

"Yes, indeed I have an obligation to treat any injured man, regardless of his transgressions." Highsmith looked at Mary and grimaced. "But you know, Grenough's cut was quite deep. In fact, at one point, the tip of the blade went right through to the skin and flesh into the mouth." He shrugged his shoulders. "And I have to admit that when I sewed the wound, it wasn't one of my best jobs. The light was bad and there was still a lot of blood flowing; that really complicated things. And then I had no assistant with me." He shook his head in evident sorrow. "I fear that my stitches were sloppily done and the esteemed Mr. Grenough is going to have a bad, disfiguring scar for the rest of his life." He looked into Mary's eyes. "I deeply regret my incompetence."

Mary looked at the surgeon, puzzled for an instant. The fact was, she knew Highsmith was extraordinarily deft with the needle. But then she suddenly understood what he was trying to tell her. She smiled warmly at him and put her hand on his arm. "Thank you for letting me know about that, Doctor."

Highsmith grinned, a twinkle in his eyes. "Quite all right, my dear. And now I have a prescription for you: Take a swig of that rum I know you have around here somewhere and then get a night's rest. It will all seem better in the morning."

* * *

The next evening, Mary sat alone on a log in front of the hospital fire. It was a chilly night and she had wrapped a blanket around her shoulders and was holding it tightly closed with her hands. Kathryn had gone over to her husband's company to visit with him. Taggart and Lister were playing cards in one of the tents with a pair of friends. Mary was just as glad to be without companionship for she was still recovering from the shock of the events at Grenough's tent and working through things in her mind. Then she looked up to see Kirkwood and Tavish walking toward her, laughing and talking as they came. She saw that Kirkwood had a haversack over his shoulder, which was curious since it was part of a soldier's marching kit but not something normally carried around camp.

The two stopped in front of the fire and looked down at her. Kirkwood grinned broadly and then glanced over at Tavish and winked. "Ian, I told you this was a good night to come visit Mary. And look at her; the most bonnie lass in the regiment sittin' here by herself with 'na a single young buck to keep her company."

Tavish smiled roguishly. "A tragedy indeed; but then, it is experienced old corporals like us who know when to come see the girls while the young privates are sittin' around just dreamin' about it."

With that, they sat down, one on either side of her. Mary laughed, suddenly glad to see her old friends. "Speaking of young bucks, I'm surprised you two haven't brought McGregor along, the way you've been trying to make us a match."

Kirkwood shrugged. "Well, the lad is out on a guard post for the night, under the tender mercies of Lieutenant Welford."

Tavish looked skyward. "And better him it is than me."

Kirkwood leaned close to Mary. "Besides, lass, this is a night for friends from the 77th. We can sit here and talk about the old days and absent mates."

Mary reached down and patted Kirkwood's haversack. "And what have you got in there, Bob?"

"Ah yes, lass. I ran into a good piece of luck which will make this a right good old night for us."

"A piece of luck, Bob? What do you mean?"

"Well, early this mornin' I was talkin' with Sergeant Leslie when the Sergeant Major comes up to us and says, "Leslie, I've got orders for a work detail and need you to provide the men: A corporal and four privates, if you will." Kirkwood made a crooked smile. "So naturally Leslie turns to me. 'Here's your man', he says."

Mary asked, "Lucky you; what was the detail?"

"We was to go over and help that man Grenough, the one who was the Indian Commissioner, pack up his baggage and get it onto pack horses. The sergeant major said he was leavin'."

Mary stiffened. "He's leaving the expedition?"

"He's gone; left before noon today."

Mary stared at Kirkwood. "Do you know why?"

Kirkwood said, "Well, their lordships didn't calculate it was necessary to take me into their confidence. But I can tell you it wasn't Grenough's idea."

Mary asked, "How do you know that?"

"Because when we got there Grenough was sittin' in front of the tent, with a bandage over the side of his face. I told him we was there to help him get packed up and he looked puzzled. He asked, 'Why do I need to pack up? Are we moving the camp again?'."

Kirkwood smiled at the other two. "So now I was puzzled and didn't know what to say. But then I heard someone behind me clear his throat. It was Lieutenant Faulkner, Colonel Bouquet's adjutant. Then he holds out a written message to Grenough and says. 'This should explain things, Mr. Grenough'."

"Grenough reads the note and looks up at Faulkner. 'This just says that Bouquet won't be needing my services anymore in negotiations and says I'm to go back to Fort Pitt with the next courier'."

"Faulkner nods and says, 'That's quite correct, sir; the colonel is confident that negotiations have progressed far enough that he can take care of things himself. He doesn't want to inconvenience you any further. The next courier is leaving about noon today. The colonel says you're to leave with him'."

Kirkwood shrugged his shoulders. "Well, Grenough shakes his head. 'Lieutenant, I really must say I do not understand. Negotiations are in fact just beginning. Perhaps I should pay a call on Henry to clear this up?' But Faulkner puts his hand up. 'No, Mr. Grenough, Colonel Bouquet thought you might want to see him, but regrets to say that he will be busy in conferences all morning and won't be able to meet with you. Sir, you are to depart forthwith'."

Tavish looked at Kirkwood. "Now that's puzzling. Word is that Bouquet and Grenough been thick as thieves since the campaign started."

Kirkwood said, "Aye, Ian, that may be true, but Faulkner stayed right there while we got Grenough's baggage packed and loaded onto horses. He was friendly an all, but it weren't no doubt in my mind he was there makin' sure Grenough didn't have 'na choice but to leave on time."

Mary's head was abuzz. She stared into the fire. *Was Bouquet's decision to send Grenough home somehow connected to her? Had Joshua told the colonel about the affair in the tent yesterday? After all, Baird had left in a hurry after she had told him the details. Had he told Bouquet despite her request to keep it all quiet?*

Then Mary's thoughts were interrupted by the sound of Kirkwood's voice. "But I have to say that His Excellency Mr. Grenough's departure is good luck for us."

Ian said, "And how is that, Bob?"

Mary looked at Tavish and then over at Kirkwood. "So, can we take it that this good fortune has something to do with that haversack, Bob?"

Kirkwood grinned roguishly and pulled the haversack onto his lap. "Indeed, it happens that it does." He opened the sack and pulled out a glass bottle, several sausages, and a loaf of bread. "Now when I was packing up Grenough, I put this bottle and sausage aside behind a log, just to get it out of the way of some other things we were packin'. I planned to ask Grenough where he wanted this stuff packed; but damned if somehow I didn't forget about it until the gentleman was on his way with the courier." He winked at his companions. "So it seems all we can do about it now is sample it to see how our betters live."

They readily followed Kirkwood's suggestion and had a merry evening.

Mary savored the whiskey. She found that it tasted even smoother and more flavorable than when it had been forced on her at the merchant's tent.

Mary smiled to herself; she was sure the enhanced taste had everything to do with the knowledge that Grenough was far away to the east on the trail back to Fort Pitt.

CHAPTER SIX

The Forest Trails

Mary stood watching as scores of soldiers from the Pennsylvania and Virginia regiments worked to raise a small village of crude cabins. Logs had been felled and were being dragged to the site by teams of pack horses pressed into service with makeshift harnesses. Most of the animals weren't used to this kind of work and were recalcitrant and hard to control. The soldiers weren't particularly used to this kind of work either, and they cursed as they attempted to keep the horses at their task. A group of men, stripped down to their shirtsleeves, were dressing and notching the logs while others teamed up to move them into place to form walls. Another group was busy cutting pine boughs and other material to form a thatch for the roofs.

Mary knew that the cabins were to house the white hostages Bouquet expected to receive from the tribes. But he also wanted a place where the surgeons and nurses of the hospital could examine the returnees and treat them for ailments and infirmities if necessary. Mary had been told that one cabin would be used as a nursery to care for young children. Moreover, Bouquet planned to keep all the refugees together so that men of the expedition would have one place to come and look for family members who had been held as hostages. Doc Highsmith had told Mary that many of the men of the Pennsylvania and Virginia battalions had enlisted in the hope of finding lost wives, children, and other relations who had been taken in either the French War or the current rebellion.

The cabins were being built just a hundred yards or so away from the edge of the Indian camp. And, in fact, the tribal camp was Mary's actual destination on this sunny October day; she wanted to talk with Abigail Gibson. Ever since the day that the fair-haired woman had come to the hospital, Mary had become obsessed with the idea of finding a way to help her learn the procedure for inoculating patients against smallpox. While Abigail's intent was to treat all the people in her village, Mary's objective was more narrow and personal: She wanted to shield the little boy who looked so much like Wend Eckert. The child's face and eyes had haunted her while she slept. Then, deep in the night, she had had a nightmare vision of the boy covered in oozing pox sores, writhing in pain and fever as he lay dying. Mary had come awake shuddering and had immediately resolved to protect the boy whatever the cost.

Now, as she watched the construction work, she searched her mind for ways to provide Abigail the necessary information. Then it suddenly came to her: She would essentially memorize the smallpox treatment procedure in Highsmith's book, then meet with Abigail at the edge of the Indian camp area to pass it to her verbally. Mary felt a lightening of her heart as she made her plan; she knew it could work. As Wend had told her, Abigail was extremely smart; surely she could remember what Mary recited to her. She turned and walked rapidly toward the demarcation line between the military and tribal camps, intending to explain her plan to Abigail and arrange for a time for them to make the exchange.

The line was marked with stakes at intervals along the ground. Sentinels were posted to ensure no unauthorized persons came into the military camp from the other side or that soldiers entered the Indian camp. Mary could see Indians of various tribes — mostly Delaware and Mingo — moving about. Shelters of various kinds had been built and women were working around the campfires. Men stood about in groups, some joking and laughing, others in serious conversation.

Mary noticed a young white man in Indian garb sitting on a stump near the stake line. He was quietly observing the military camp. Mary judged him to be in his early twenties. He was tanned and had dark, almost black hair, but clearly was white. She thought: Perhaps I can prevail upon him to find Abigail.

She walked until she was just across the stake line from where he sat. She waved to attract his attention. "Hello, sir!"

The youth slowly turned his head to look at her and spent a few seconds moving his eyes up and down her body.

Mary asked, "Do you speak English?"

The man laughed. "Of course; I ain't been a captive so long I forgot." Then he shrugged his shoulders. "But then, there are indeed those who have lost the old tongue." He smiled at Mary. "What's your name?"

"Mary Fraser. I'm with the hospital." She waved toward the log cabins. "We'll be looking you over after the exchange."

The man smiled broadly and inspected Mary again. "Now I won't mind that a bit if you're the one who looks me over."

Mary laughed. "Well, you are a saucy one, aren't you?"

"I speak my mind." His eyes twinkled as he looked at her.

"What's your name?" she asked.

"My white name is Simon. Simon Girty. I was taken back in '56 when a war party captured Fort Granville in the Juniata Valley."

"So you've been with the Indians for eight years?" She thought a moment. "Are you with the Delaware or Mingo?"

"I been with the Delaware and Mingo. But mostly with the Mingo, or as you might call them, the Seneca."

"Well, Simon, I'm glad to hear that, because the truth is, I'm looking for another person who is with the Mingo. She's a white hostage they call Orenda. She's a blond woman who has a white son about five years old."

Girty nodded. "I know her; fact is, everyone knows about Orenda. She's the Medicine Woman of the Slippery Rock Creek Mingo. But I met her personally a couple of times and saw the child." Girty shook his head. "The boy is the son of the man she was with before she was captured."

Mary smiled. "Yes, that's right. Her man is named Wend Eckert; he's German."

Girty put his head back and laughed. "You may know him as Eckert, but he's known in every village in the Ohio Country as 'The Scalp Stealer.' And he's considered a great coward."

"Wend Eckert is a very brave man. Why do the Indians think he's such a coward?"

Girty cocked his head. "That's 'cause he took all the scalps of his family right off the Slippery Rock Creek Mingoes' trophy rack while the people of the village were held back by the bayonets of British soldiers. He didn't get them because of any valor of his own. Now every Mingo wants to be the one to take his scalp. But the one who wants to do it most is Wolf Claw, the war captain of the Slippery Rock Creek village."

Mary shuddered at the thought. But she needed to turn the conversation back to Abigail. "Look, Simon, I need to talk to Orenda. It's about medical business. Can you find her for me and ask her to come here?"

Girty shook his head and gave Mary a crooked smile. "And here all this time I thought you was interested in me." He paused and screwed up his face. "But I'd be glad to find Orenda for you." He looked back into the Indian camp, then back at Mary. "Except there be one large problem: The Slippery Rock Creek Mingo left camp today, headed back toward their village."

Mary was shocked. "Why did they do that?"

"Because they don't want to give up Orenda; their elders and Wolf Claw, who is her husband, have vowed they'd never let her be returned to the whites. And the word is, Orenda don't want to go anyway." Girty paused and stared at Mary.

"And I can tell you, they ain't the only ones who won't give up their adopted whites. There's other bands which have been leaving the camp since the rumor started that the English will demand that all the captives be given back."

Mary nodded. "Mr. Girty, I can understand that. But how long ago did the Slippery Rock Mingo leave?"

Girty looked thoughtful for a moment. "Not long; maybe an hour ago."

Mary stamped her foot in frustration. She had missed her opportunity. She sighed and looked at Girty. "Thank you for your help. I've enjoyed talking with you, sir." She turned and started to walk back toward the hospital. From behind, she heard Girty call out, "I'll being seeing you after the treaty for that examination!"

Mary waved back at the youth without turning and kept on her way.

She hadn't gone another ten steps when the idea came to her. There was still a way to get the smallpox information to Abigail. It would be against regulations and she couldn't do it alone; she would need Joshua's help. But would he take the chance? If he knew it would help Wend's son, maybe he would. But there was only one way to tell. Mary set off as fast as she could walk to find the scout.

She caught up with Joshua at the horse picket line, grooming Beau. He greeted her with his characteristic grin and good humor. "Hello, lass; it's lookin like a fine October day with a good fall sun shinin' down on us."

Mary didn't waste any time on pleasantries. "Joshua, do you think Beau could carry the two of us for a ways?"

Baird stopped grooming with the brush still resting on the horse's side and turned to look at the girl. "He could, well as any horse in the camp. You lookin' for a pleasure ride today?" He waved toward the camp perimeter. "Of course, the camp guards might have a little problem with us riding out into the bush, seein' as only people with military business are allowed through the lines."

"It's not a pleasure ride, Joshua. I want to take some medical information to Abigail Gibson. It's about smallpox inoculation." She put her hand on Baird's arm. "Joshua, it's for Wend Eckert's son and we don't have a lot of time."

Baird's face wrinkled up in puzzlement. "Whoa, girl! You're all excited and not makin' a lot of sense. How did you get tied in with Abigail? And why do you need to help her son? And what's all the hurry?"

Mary took a deep breath and organized her thoughts. Then, speaking slowly, she told Joshua the whole story. She finished by saying, "So you see, I need to get the instructions about inoculations to Abigail to make sure that Wend's son is protected."

Joshua stared at her for a long time. Then he shook his head. "Lass, you still got it bad for Eckert — just when you should be figurin' out how to put him behind you and be gettin' on with your life."

"Yes, I know I must come to grips with my feelings. But you'll help me, won't you?" She looked at him beseechingly. "For God's sake, please help me with this Joshua."

Baird sighed heavily, then nodded slowly. "I'm probably goin' to regret it, but of course I'll help." He put his brush down. "I'll get saddled right now."

"Thank you," Mary said. "I have to go back to the hospital and get something." Then her mind raced on. "But how will we get through the guards?"

Baird smiled conspiratorially. "It'll have to be done very carefully. But just leave that to me. You go get your stuff and meet me behind the 2nd Pennsylvania tents. Be there soon as you can."

Mary walked rapidly to the hospital. She looked around; Kathryn was standing by the tent where a couple of sick men were laying, exchanging pleasantries with them; the two orderlies were talking and paid her no attention. Neither surgeon was anywhere to be seen. She slipped into Munro's tent and grabbed the medical reference book. She laid it on his writing table and opened it to the pages where the procedure for smallpox inoculation was discussed. There were three pages giving background and then a recommended method. She took a scalpel from Munro's bag and carefully sliced out each of the pages as close to the binding as she could manage. Then she closed the book and looked at it critically; she was satisfied that there was virtually no visible evidence that pages were missing. She sighed; sooner or later Munro would discover the mutilation; but it might be weeks, for he rarely looked at the book. She would deal with his retribution when, and if, the situation arose. Quickly she put the book back where she had found it and, folding the papers into a packet, put them in a secure place in her gown. She looked around the tent, making sure everything was as it had been, then furtively slipped out through the flap. It had all taken less than two minutes.

Feeling like the thief she was, Mary hurried to the camp of the Pennsylvanians. She found Baird, rifle over his shoulder on a sling, holding his horse by the reins and talking to another man. As she got closer, she realized it was Lieutenant Colonel Clayton, the commandant of the 2nd Battalion. She approached hesitantly until Joshua waved her to join them.

The scout said, "Mary, say hello to my good friend Asher Clayton."

In deference to his rank, Mary gave Clayton a curtsy and bid him good morning.

Clayton looked Mary over. "Well, Miss Fraser, in consideration of our former companion Wend Eckert, we two veterans of the Paxton Militia have formed a small conspiracy to get you out through the lines here. It happens that the guards at this point are from my battalion and I've notified them to give you no trouble." He gave a glance to Joshua. "They'll swear they never saw you ride out. But if you don't return before tomorrow morning when our men are relieved by another battalion, I'm afraid you'll be on your own coming back."

Baird nodded. "If we find the correct trail, we should be back in a few hours. Anyway, we'll deal with that later." He gave Clayton a jab on the shoulder and said, "Thanks, Asher." Then he turned and mounted; Mary noticed he made a grimace as he raised his left leg to the stirrup. He turned and offered her a hand up and she made herself as comfortable as she could behind him.

Clayton stepped over, put his hand on the side of the horse and grinned up at Joshua and then at Mary. "Someday we must have to have a serious talk with Eckert about how he gets all these women to be so loyal. He's married to Peggy McCartie, the prettiest woman of Sherman Valley, and now here's another beautiful girl determined to help the son he had by a third woman." He shook his head. "I confess I don't know how he does it."

Mary looked down, gave him her broadest grin and said, "If you were a woman, you'd know."

And with that, Joshua spurred Beau forward and they were off. Mary looked back to see Clayton standing with his hands on his hips, laughing as he watched them go.

* * *

They passed a posting of Pennsylvania Regiment guards without stopping, Joshua simply waving at the sergeant in charge of the position. The forest contained many large trees but the underbrush was light enough so the horse faced little obstruction and they were able to move fast.

Over his shoulder Joshua told Mary, "There's a trail ahead which goes pretty much north-east. It's the most likely path the Mingo would follow; it will take them to a concentration of villages on the upper Beaver called the Kuskuskies; then after they cross the stream at that point another path will take them eastward along Slippery Rock Creek to their village." He paused and maneuvered Beau around a thicket. Then he continued, "We'll head northward 'till we cut the path."

In fact they came upon the trail in less than a quarter-hour after passing the guard position. Joshua slipped to the ground and passed the reins up to Mary. "Hold him here while I scout the sign on the trail."

Mary watched as Baird walked eastward along the path, looking at the ground, sometimes stopping and kneeling as he examined sign. Then he walked off the path for a short distance and examined something near a group of thick bushes. Shortly he made his way back to the trail and motioned for Mary to bring the horse up to him.

Joshua mounted, and once again groaned and strained lifting the left foot up to the stirrup. He looked back at Mary and said, "This damn hip of mine; I hate to admit it, but its getting' worse." He grimaced. "Wend keeps tellin' me I ought to be sittin' on a chair in front of the fire; but I'll be damned if I'm going to let this leg tie me down. I got lots of good years in me yet."

Mary said soothingly, "Of course you do, Joshua. It's hardly slowing you down."

"Damn right, lass!"

"So what did you see on the trail?"

"Sure 'nough there's been a big group of Indians heading along this path. Lots of moccasin tracks of all sizes — it means warriors, women, and children. They got a couple of horses with them carrying their goods. And someone relieved their bowels beside the trail. Not too long ago, either, 'cause the pile is still warm." He looked up the trail. "We should catch 'em pretty soon."

But a few miles further on, they came to a fork in the trail. Joshua had to dismount and search the ground all over again.

Mary said, "I thought you said the original trail would take them toward their village; shouldn't we stay on that?"

"This branch takes them up to the Great Trail; it's a bit longer, but it will also take them in the right direction. It's wider and might be easier travelin' for their women and children and horses."

Baird nosed around some more, then came back to mount Beau. "Nope; they stayed with the direct trail. Let's go."

It took them not more than another hour to catch up, for the Mingo were on foot and encumbered with their women and children. But then Joshua didn't dare push Beau too hard, given the extra load he was carrying. He was also very cautious, stopping several more times to look around.

The first time Mary asked in frustration, "Why are we stopping? We know they're ahead of us."

"We're stopping to scout around, 'cause them Mingo are going to be prickly 'bout anybody comin' up behind them real fast on horseback. They know Bouquet's got troops of light horse and peace ain't been declared yet. They may figure he's tryin' to keep them from leavin' the meeting ground." He remounted again and said, "If they hear us comin', they might lay some sort of ambush for us if were not careful."

In fact, they eventually rode around a bend and suddenly encountered two warriors standing in the trail, their firelocks at the ready.

Joshua pulled up the horse and said quietly, "There be other warriors concealed in the bush on either side of the trail and its sure they got guns aimed at us. And all their women and children are hidin' down the trail." He nodded to the two men in the path and whispered, "The taller one is Wolf Claw himself."

At that moment Wolf Claw pointed at Joshua and spoke up in broken English. "You I know; you are one they call Baird. You spy for the British. Why you ride here with a woman?" He motioned to Mary and scowled. "Does the Colonel Bouquet send women to spy on the Mingo now?"

Joshua slid down from the saddle and walked up to the two warriors. "Bouquet didn't send us; we came on our own to talk to the Mingo of Slippery Rock Creek. This woman carries something the Mingo would want to have."

Wolf Claw cocked his head and again pointed to Joshua, his finger just inches from the scout's face. "You came to our village; came this same time last year with many soldiers. Scalp Stealer was with you then. Why is Scalp Stealer not with you now? Where is the man who stole our scalps?"

"He is not with the army. He is at his home."

"Ha! So Scalp Stealer has no heart to face the Mingo. He stays behind with the women." Wolf Claw turned to the warrior beside him and said something in the Seneca tongue; the man laughed. Then he called out something and people started to come out of the forest. He looked back at Joshua and then pointed to Mary. "Mingo have no need for anything from woman with red hair. We go."

Mary was shaking in frustration. She looked up the path, and but couldn't see Abigail. She knew the woman must be near; she couldn't constrain herself any longer and shouted out: "Abigail! Abigail Gibson! I have what you wanted from the hospital!" Then she immediately realized she should have used the girl's Mingo name.

But suddenly Abigail emerged from the cover of the bush, not thirty feet away. She walked back toward the group on the trail, saying something in Seneca to Wolf Claw.

Mary climbed down from the horse and quickly walked to meet her.

Abigail stood looking at Mary for a long moment, a frown on her face. Then she asked in a sharp tone, "How do you know my English name? I never told you."

Mary gathered her thoughts to explain, but before she could say anything Abigail pointed at her; the woman's eyes were a piercing, steely blue as she stared at Mary's clothing.

"My God, where did you get that gown?"

Mary had forgotten she was wearing the blue traveling gown. She sighed. "Yes, it was yours, Abigail. I found it in your wagon a day after you were captured. Wend Eckert said I could have it."

More surprise registered on Abigail's face. "You know Wend?"

"Yes, I do. My mother and I were with the army company which found him lying on the road after the massacre. We tended his wounds."

While she was speaking, Wend's son had come out from hiding and had come up beside his mother, grabbing her linen shift with his hand. She put her hand on his shoulder.

Mary smiled at the boy and then at Abigail. She reached into her gown and pulled out the packet of pages from the medical book. "Here, I brought you this; it's the instructions for performing smallpox inoculations."

Abigail took the papers, looked at them for a moment, and then stared at Mary in puzzlement. "Won't you get in trouble? Why are you doing this for the Mingo?"

Mary motioned to the little boy. "I'm doing it to keep Wend's flesh and blood safe."

Abigail shook her head. "I still don't understand. Why are you so concerned about him?"

Mary smiled at her. "Wend told me you were very smart. But you're not acting that way right now, Abigail." She looked directly into her eyes. "The truth is this: We each shared one brief moment of intimacy with Wend and we both wish it could have extended for a lifetime."

Abigail's mouth opened wide, then her face transformed into a knowing look. She nodded and said, "Yes, I understand." But almost immediately the smile was replaced with another look of puzzlement. "If you're so in love with Wend, why aren't you with him now?"

"Because, by a twist of fate, he thought I was dead and he married another woman. He's with her now in Virginia and they're about to have a child."

Abigail nodded; then a look of concern came over her face. She quickly looked down at her little boy and sighed. "I'm glad you've told me what has become of Wend. But I wonder if he will keep and cherish the memory of our son, now that he's raising a family of his own."

Joshua had quietly moved closer to the two women and now he spoke up. "Don't ever doubt it, Miss Gibson. I know personal-like that he is upset 'cause he won't see the little lad grow up."

"I'm glad to hear that, Mr. Baird."

At that moment, Wolf Claw called out loudly and harshly to Abigail in Seneca and impatiently motioned for her to start moving up the trail. She spun on him and spoke back in a tenor as harsh as he had used to her; Wolf Claw visibly recoiled at her scolding.

Hearing the tone of her words, Mary thought to herself: *Abigail is not a woman you would want to have angry with you.*

Then Abigail looked at Mary and said, "We must go now; but I'll always be indebted to you." And with that she turned and followed the others trudging eastward along the trail.

Wolf Claw called out loudly and several warriors emerged from cover and followed in the wake of the other villagers. Soon Wolf Claw stood alone, looking at Joshua. Then he smirked and said, "You tell the Scalp Stealer to stay by the hearth with his women. If he return to land of the Mingo, he is a dead man."

Joshua answered in Seneca; he talked at some length, and when he finished Wolf Claw simply gave him a scowl and then turned and walked away up the path.

Mary asked, "What did you tell him?"

"I just said that a lot of men had tried to kill Wend and most of them are now in their graves."

"You talked longer than that, Joshua."

"Well, I put things in a little more detail than I told you. Just to make sure 'ole Wolf Claw got the right idea about how things would go if he ran into Wend."

Mary nodded; then she stared after the departing Mingoes, a thoughtful look on her face. Then she said, "You know, Joshua, that Abigail is tall and pretty but she is so unemotional. And those piercing blue eyes make her seem cold as ice. I can't understand why Wend found her so attractive."

Baird looked at her for a long moment. Then his face broke into a wolfish grin. "If you was a man, you'd understand."

* * *

"Climb on down, Mary," Joshua said. "It's time to rest Beau again." Then Baird dismounted also and prepared to lead the horse.

"Where are we?" Mary asked. How long 'till we have to cross the guard lines?"

"We're comin' up on that split in the trail we saw on the way out."

"That means we're less than an hour from camp."

Joshua nodded. He said, "We got to hurry to make sure we return by the same guards that we passed this morning." Then he suddenly put his hand up in a signal to stay quiet. He whispered, "It may be I hear somethin'." He dropped flat and put his ear to the ground.

Mary went to her knees beside him and kept as quiet as she could manage.

Baird raised himself to his knees and said softly, "Horses; a lot of them, to the north; I think they're comin' down the trail from the Great Path."

She looked at him. "Could it be a patrol of our light horse?"

"Naw; there weren't no plan to send them out. And if they were out, they'd more like to be patrolling further to the west, lookin' to see if the Shawnee were comin' in for talks or gatherin' for a fight."

Mary stood up. "What are we to do?"

"I'm gonna' see who it is." He looked around. "We'll tie Beau here out of sight in the bush and you can stay with him, where you'll be safe. I'll go on up to the forks and see who this be."

"No I'm not staying behind, Joshua. I'd be fearful alone out here. I can stay quiet; I want to go with you."

Exasperation crossed Baird's face. Then he shrugged his shoulders. "All right, but don't say a word, no matter what happens. And you better stay still where I put you."

It took the two only a few minutes to reach the forks on foot. Joshua quickly found them good cover where they could hide and still see the trail. They lay side by side on the ground amidst a dense thicket.

They had made it to cover just in time. Almost immediately Mary began to hear the sound of shod hooves. She thought: *That probably means white men.* Soon the horses were close and she could feel them through the ground.

In another few minutes a single horse and rider came into sight. The man was dressed in a hunting shirt and leggings. He held a longrifle balanced across the pommel in front of him. His scruffy beard and hair, visible under a broad-brimmed hat, was jet black. The rider seemed familiar to Mary, but she couldn't quite place him. It was only a minute or two more until a long pack train appeared. And Mary almost broke her promise of silence by gasping when she recognized the man leading the first string of horses. It was the hulking waggoner with the disfigured face who had been with Grenough on the day the hospital wagon had crashed into the gully! He was dressed in similar fashion to the other man and also carried a rifle.

Then Mary realized who the black-haired man on the point was — Grenough's chief retainer, the Irishman named McCrae. Mary kept watching as another string of horses came by and thought the man leading the horses also looked familiar. Then she paid attention to the packs on the horses; all were covered by canvas, but many of had shapes under the covers which could only be wooden kegs. Mary realized the train was carrying a great amount of black powder. Soon another man leading a third string, consisting of only four animals, passed their positon. She figured that was the provisions and baggage for the men in the train. And finally, another single rider came past, acting as the rear guard. Mary quickly assessed what she had seen: At least twenty-four pack horses and five mounted, armed men. All in all, it was quite a train and obviously full of illicit war materials. As they watched, the train came to the fork and took the trail heading westward. In ten minutes, it was out of sight and quiet had returned to the forest.

Joshua pushed himself up from the ground and reached down to help Mary. "We got to get back to the horse and make time back to camp." He turned and headed toward where Beau was tethered.

Mary exclaimed, "Wait Joshua — I recognized some of those men! The black haired point man and the man with the broken face were traveling with Grenough on the way to Fort Pitt back in September."

"I've no doubt you're right, lass." Joshua scrunched up his face. "That man with the bad face is named Matt Bratton; he's worked for Grenough for years. I know him well; he's from Sherman Valley. He's a bully who used to give Wend trouble all the time."

Suddenly Mary remembered what Grenough had told her. "Yes, yes! Grenough did tell me his name was Bratton." Then she remembered something else Grenough had mentioned and her mind connected it with what Baird had just said. Suddenly she felt a cold knot in her stomach. "Joshua, was it Wend who ruined that man's face in a fight? In a tavern?"

Joshua broke into a wide grin. "Oh, yeah, lass, that he did; and I can tell you it was a beautiful thing to see. First time ever I saw Wend lose his temper. He knocked Bratton over with a wooden stool and then beat his face with a log from the hearth." He winked at Mary. "Truth is, he would have killed Bratton if I hadn't stopped him."

Mary said, "Grenough said the fight was over some tart. How was Wend involved in something like that?"

Suddenly Joshua's face turned grim. "She weren't no tart, though Bratton called her that. It was Peggy McCartie, the woman Wend married. Wend lit into Bratton 'cause he called her a whore."

Mary looked at Joshua's face and instinctively knew there was more to the story than he was telling her, but also realized this wasn't the time to get into it all. Instead she said, "The real point is that McCrae and Bratton work for Grenough and they're out here taking supplies to the Indians."

Joshua nodded, then said, "You remember back at Pitt when I told you there was a traitor with the expediton? Well, the man was Grenough. He's the power behind a big outlaw trading ring. Wend figured that out last year. And I ain't got no doubt he's organized what we just saw."

"My God, and I thought he was such a great man." Then another thought hit her and she glared at Baird. "Why didn't you tell me who it was that first night at Fort Pitt? Why didn't you go to Bouquet right away?"'

"For the same reason you didn't want to report Grenough after he attacked you in his tent. He's so powerful and so tight with important men that it's hard to make anyone believe what he's been doing. I needed to figure out how to do it." Joshua's grimaced. "It weren't 'till he attacked you that I got the gumption to go to Bouquet. That night, after I took you back to the fire, I went straight to the colonel and laid out everything to him."

Mary's angered flared. "So you thought you couldn't trust me? You thought I wouldn't keep quiet?"

"No, Mary, it's not . . .'"

Mary cut him off. "For God's sake, if you had told me, I could have avoided Grenough." She stamped her foot. "Joshua, I still have nightmares about that man pulling me onto his lap and sticking his hand down my breast; I wake up in the night sweating."

"Now lass, I can't take back what be done an' gone; wish I could. But you got to believe I figured it was best not to tell you, so you wouldn't be involved in any way." He waved his hands. "And how was I to know Grenough had taken a shine to you?"

"All right, all right; I believe you. Anyway, we can't do anything about it now." Mary crossed her arms and stood in the path, cooling down. Then another thought came to her. "So that's why Bouquet sent Grenough away so abruptly?"

"Yes. I still didn't have no hard evidence to give Bouquet, but he believed me 'cause of all the time we been working together and saw how logically Grenough fit into the picture. And he knowed from last year that Wend was lookin' to find the people who killed his family. So he decided to cut Grenough out of all the negotiations with the tribes and send him back east."

Mary hurried to keep up and shouted, "Hey, what do we do about what we just saw? We aren't supposed to be out here. How do we explain it?"

"There ain't no choice, Mary: We got to come clean. Right now we got to get to Bouquet fast as we can and tell him 'bout this train. There was a lot of damn powder and lead in those packs. If the Shawnees get it, they might just start the war up all over again."

Joshua led Beau out of the bush and reached up to stroke his muzzle and then his mane. He said to the big bay, "We're gonna' need everything you got for the next hour, Old Man, even though you're carryin' double."

Mary looked at Joshua caressing the animal. She asked in a doubtful tone, "Do you think he understands what you want from him?"

Baird looked back at her and grinned with pride. "Oh, yeah. He's got as much heart as I ever seen in any horse." Then he swung up into the saddle and reached down to give her a hand. "Time you got aboard and we were out of here." He pulled her up to her place behind the saddle and then turned and said, "We got to get to camp as fast as possible and make sure we don't overtake that train on the trail ahead. So we'll have to go directly through the bush; it's pretty open hereabouts, but we will have to be careful."

Then he touched Beau's sides and they started out. After maybe 100 yards, he turned the horse off the trail into the trees. When possible, Baird brought the horse up to the gallop, and Mary could feel the hunter's great power as they swept through the woodland. At first the pace frightened her, with trees whipping past them, but Joshua and the horse worked in concert to ensure Beau's hooves stayed on clear ground. Now and again he had to step over roots and sometimes make short leaps to clear concentrations of exposed roots or other objects on the ground. But after a while Mary came to trust the horse's surefootedness and her anxiety diminished.

In less than half an hour they had smoke from campfires visible against the sky and that helped guide them in the right direction. Joshua called back, "With all the maneuvering we been doin', I ain't got any real idea where we are along the lines of the camp; I ain't sure where Asher's guards are posted. So we're just goin' to head right in. We're pretty damn close now."

It was just a few minutes later that disaster struck. Beau took a jump over a large fallen log, much like several others they had encountered. But on the other side was a piled-up tangle of dead branches which Joshua didn't see. The big horse caught a front hoof on the debris and in a split second he went over.

As the horse stumbled, Joshua exclaimed, "Oh, shit!"

The last thing Mary remembered was being catapulted into the air and the sound of a woman's scream. Then everything went black.

CHAPTER SEVEN
The Raid

Mary opened her eyes to find the afternoon sun nearly blinding her with its intensity. She blinked and shut her eyes again. Close by a highland voice said "Corporal, I think the lass is 'na bad hurt; she's waking up."

Mary again opened her eyes. A young private of the 42nd, a man she didn't know, was kneeling beside her. She looked around and saw Joshua on his feet, talking with a corporal. Two other privates were standing by, listening. Baird was bleeding from cuts on his face, but otherwise seemed all right.

The scout said in a beseeching tone of voice, "For God's sake, corporal, we've got to go see Colonel Bouquet; I've got some news for him what won't wait."

The corporal shot back, "I told you already, I sent for the outpost officer. He'll decide what to do with you when he gets here."

Baird turned and walked over to where Mary lay and knelt beside her. "Lass, how are you doing?"

"I don't know yet, Joshua. Help me get up and then I'll tell you."

Joshua stood up and gave Mary his hand. She pulled herself up to her feet. She had some pain in her right leg and shoulder and there was a sharp stinging on her face. But there didn't seem to be anything broken.

The private she had first seen said, "Miss, you got some scratches on your face."

Mary put her hand up to her cheek and came away with blood smeared across her palm and fingers.

Meanwhile, Joshua had gone over to examine Beau. The horse was down on his side, but his eyes were open and he was moving. Baird knelt by the animal for a minute, then stood up holding the reins. "Come on, fellow, try to get up." Beau raised his head, and then with a mighty effort struggled to his hooves, leaves and twigs falling off of him.

The big hunter whinnied in pain as he rose.

Baird stroked the animal's mane. "It's alright, boy; I'd be surprised if you didn't hurt after that fall." He led the horse forward, and Mary could see that Beau limped on his right foreleg.

Then one of the privates called out, "Corporal, here's the lieutenant."

Mary looked back toward the camp to see Lieutenant Welford. He was in the cut-down uniform of the 60th she had tailored for him and carried a fusil in his hand. A sergeant walked beside him.

All the troops of the outpost came to attention.

Welford said, "Corporal, I'll have your explanation for what is going on here."

"I'm na' sure, sir. We heard a woman scream, then a loud crash just outside the lines, sir. So we came to investigate. Found that horse down, this here scout sitting on the ground holding his head, and the woman lying unconscious in front of the horse." He paused and motioned toward Mary. "The lass, she came awake just a minute ago."

Joshua spoke up. "Lieutenant Welford, you know who I am. I found out somethin' I need to tell Bouquet right now."

"Yes Baird, I know who you are. But I don't know what you are doing outside the lines with a young camp girl. I've not been informed that anyone was coming through the lines." He pursed his lips and looked over the two of them. "I do know one thing: Something is not right here."

"For God's sake, Welford, just take us to the colonel. He'll understand everything once I give him my report."

"What I understand, Baird, is that Colonel Bouquet has issued orders requiring that everyone stay within the confines of the camp and requiring strict enforcement by the guards. And I do intend to enforce those orders." He turned to the soldiers. "Sergeant, you and I and one of these privates will escort these two people to the senior guard officer." He pointed to Beau. "Corporal, that horse's leg is severely hurt. Destroy the animal."

A look of horror came over Joshua's face. "You'll damn well not kill that horse until I've had a chance to look over the leg. He's my own property, not some army nag."

The corporal looked at Beau and said, "Lieutenant, I don't think the horse is that bad off. Maybe one of the men could lead him into the camp. There be plenty of men there who know 'bout horses."

Welford scowled. "Damn, does no one in the 42nd listen to orders? I bloody well grew up in the saddle and I say he's damaged beyond saving. Look at how he's limping." Welford quickly passed his fusil to the sergeant, marched up to the horse, pulled a large pistol from his belt, and without hesitation fired a shot into

Beau's head just below his left ear. The hunter collapsed almost instantly. He declared loudly, "There, that's settled."

Mary had never seen such fury as registered in Joshua's eyes. "You bastard! You done that just out of spite. But you just made the biggest mistake of your life." And without saying anything else, Joshua launched himself at Welford.

But he had only made it two paces before the corporal stepped forward and stuck his leg out, tripping the scout and sending him crashing to the ground. The corporal, a hulking man, went to one knee on Joshua's back, pinning him in place. He whispered, "Lay still Baird; you hit Welford and he'll have you under the lash 'afore you can blink."

Welford stuck the pistol into his belt and took his fusil back from the sergeant. He said formally, "Sergeant, put these people under discipline and let us proceed to the officer of the guard."

* * *

With Welford leading, the guard detail marched Mary and Joshua into the outlying area of the camp, heading for the post of the day's officer of the guard.

Mary felt overwhelming despair at what had happened. She turned to Joshua and said quietly, "I'm sorry that my rashness led you into such trouble. And I got your beautiful horse killed."

Joshua was still glaring at Welford with hatred in his eyes. Without breaking his stare at the officer, he replied, "Don't you fret, lass; this ain't over yet. It ain't over by a longshot. You did what you thought was right by your own lights and I agreed to help you. Far as I'm concerned, the only one who should be worryin' is Welford." He gritted his teeth. "Sooner or later we're going to get to an officer with some brains in his head."

Joshua's prediction came true in just a few minutes.

As they were passing along the outer perimeter of the 42nd camp area, the group came upon Captain Stirling and his company sergeant, Leslie, engaged in conversation. Stirling had a sheet of paper in his hand and was obviously discussing plans for the day with his sergeant. Stirling looked up and saw the group; a look of puzzlement came over his face.

After exchanging salutes with Welford, Stirling motioned the lieutenant to stop. "What have we here, Mr. Welford? Why are these people under guard?"

"They were apprehended outside the lines without proper authority, sir. Naturally, I put them under restraint and I'm taking them to the officer of the guard to determine their disposition."

In a dry tone Stirling responded, "*Naturally*, Mr. Welford. Now, can I assume that after serving as the colonel's adjutant, you recognized that Mr. Baird is the chief scout of the expedition?"

"Oh yes, sir."

"I presume you asked him what business he had outside the lines?"

Welford motioned toward Joshua. "He just keeps saying that he wants to see the colonel and that he has urgent information for him. However, I'm suspicious since he had this camp woman along with him. I took it as most irregular, sir. Especially since I had no notification that he had business outside the camp, sir. In any case, regulations specify that I should take the case to the guard officer."

Joshua stamped his foot. "Captain Stirling, for God's sake listen; the fact is, I got some news for the colonel 'bout the campaign. If I waste time repeatin' it with every officer between Welford and Bouquet, we may miss out on a big opportunity. The colonel's got to act fast."

Stirling nodded to Joshua. "I acknowledge what you say, Mr. Baird." Then he looked at Mary. "And what is your name, Miss?"

Mary curtsied and said, "Mary Fraser, nurse at the 42nd hospital, sir."

Stirling's face broke into a grin and a twinkle came into his eyes. "Oh yes, indeed I have heard of you." He touched his bonnet to her. "May I say that aside from the blood on your face, you are as refreshingly lovely as I've been told."

Mary felt herself flushing in embarrassment at Stirling's gallantry and curtsied.

Stirling touched his bonnet in response and bowed slightly, then continued. "But, Miss Fraser, I must ask: What were you doing outside the lines on this occasion?"

Mary bit her lip. She looked at Joshua for a moment, then said, "Sir, I was taking some medical information to Miss Abigail Gibson, a hostage of the Mingo Indians. Joshua agreed to help me slip out through the lines without being seen by the guards."

Joshua looked at her and she caught a slight wink.

The captain's eyes opened wide. He looked over at Joshua, then exchanged a glance with Leslie. "Mary Fraser, daughter of the 42nd and the lovely Miss Abigail Gibson, late member of Philadelphia's most elegant society, face-to- face in the wilds of Ohio; now I would have given a pretty purse to witness that!"

Stirling reflected a moment and then nodded to himself. He said to no one in particular, "This is all very intriguing; damned if I don't' want to hear the whole story." He turned to Welford. "Lieutenant, Mr. Baird guided me through the Ohio Country for six weeks last year. I have the utmost confidence in his judgment. And based on that I intend we should take him directly to see Colonel Bouquet."

Welford reared up. "You may have confidence in him sir, but procedures specify that I take him to the officer of the guard. And I intend to do so; I would be remiss in my duty if I took any other action."

Stirling raised his eyebrows. "Mr. Welford, can it possibly have escaped your memory that I am your company commander?"

Welford set his jaw. "But sir, when I am assigned to guard detail, I am required to report to the guard officer, not my company chain of command. Certainly that is clear in regulations. Therefore I must protest your plan."

"Welford, perhaps you might note that we happen to be in the bush country of Ohio, not mounting guard at the palace in London."

Welford started to speak again, but Stirling cut him off with a quick motion of his hand. He turned to Leslie and said, "Sergeant, go to the officer of the guard and inform him we're taking Mr. Baird and this young lady to headquarters. I will personally take responsibility and brief him on the details later." He looked sharply at Welford. "I believe the guard officer will fully understand my actions."

* * *

"Captain Stirling, what's this about?" Colonel Henry Bouquet sat inside his tent, sheltered from the wind, while he worked on correspondence due to go out with the next courier back to Fort Pitt. He was dressed in his full uniform, with the exception of a hat, and wore a set of spectacles across his nose. His adjutant had announced the captain, and Stirling ushered the group — Baird, Mary and Welford — within the canvas walls.

Mary looked around the tent. Bouquet's headquarters were quite austere; a camp cot, with a small folding table beside it, a camp desk and chair, and two small chests which held his personal baggage. There were considerable writing materials on the desk and a stack of papers piled on one end.

Stirling motioned toward Lieutenant Welford. "Mr. Welford was commanding a guard outpost on the north side of the camp today and apprehended Mr. Baird and Miss Fraser returning from," he hesitated a moment, "Shall we say, a personal mission, out in the bush. The Lieutenant will give you the details."

Bouquet looked at Joshua and Mary, then back to his former adjutant. "Well, Mr. Welford, what is the story?"

"One of my posts heard the hoof beats of a horse rapidly approaching the lines. Then there was a woman's scream about fifty yards out into the bush, sir. They went to investigate and found a fallen horse and these two lying on the ground. Baird was just getting up and the woman was unconscious." He paused and looked around the group. "They had no authorization to be out of the camp sir. So when the woman regained consciousness, I took them into custody to present them to the officer of the guard. Mr. Baird kept saying he wanted to see you with some urgent information; I thought the whole thing suspicious and that the officer of the guard was the proper person to sort it all out." Welford nodded toward Stirling. "On our way, Captain Stirling encountered us. We had conversations, and it came out that the woman was taking information to a band of Mingoes with the assistance of Mr. Baird."

Bouquet raised his eyebrows and looked at Stirling, then over to Joshua. "Perhaps we should hear the whole story. Why don't you tell me, Joshua?"

Mary had watched Joshua fretting as the military officers discussed the case. Now he could hold his frustration no longer. "Henry, damn it, why we was out of the lines ain't important right now. What's important is we saw a pack train of powder, a lot of it, on the way to the west, bound for the Scioto, I'll wager."

Bouquet jumped up from his chair. "The devil you say! How did they get here? How many pack animals did you see?"

"At least 24 pack horses, Colonel. From the look of it, they was carrying mostly powder, but it's sure they had lead, too. And if they was loaded like that wagon Wend Eckert blew up back in June, out on Forbes Road north of Lyttleton, they had hatchet and knife blades also." He waved at Mary. "Miss Fraser was right there with me and saw it all."

Mary nodded. "Joshua's telling the truth; I saw 24 pack horses and five men, Colonel."

Joshua continued, "They was comin' down a side trail from the Great Path, sir. I 'spect they crossed the Allegheny up towards Kittanning and took various trails to the Kuskuskies, then followed the Great Path all the way to here." He paused a second. "I figure they're carrying the stuff to the Shawnee, Colonel."

Stirling exclaimed, "Damn, Colonel; that may be why most of the Shawnee haven't come in to the negotiations. They're waiting for the ammunition they need for war."

Joshua put up his hand. "I think it's a little more complicated than that; I'd wager that stuff is going direct to Charlot Kaske. It's no secret the Shawnee chiefs are sittin' on the fence. Charlot Kaske's trying to convince them to make war. If he can show up at a council fire with a big supply of powder and lead and a lot of young hotheaded warriors behind him, he can sway them to his way of thinkin'."

Bouquet nodded. "I think you're absolutely right, Joshua. So if we can stop that train and capture the supplies, the Shawnee chiefs will come in for talks. They'll have to!"

Joshua nodded, "I don't doubt it, Colonel."

"How long ago did you see the train, Joshua?"

"No more than two hours ago, Colonel. They can't be but a few miles down the trail."

Bouquet strode out under the fly of his tent and shouted for his adjutant. "Faulkner! Lieutenant Faulkner! Come here, sir!"

The young adjutant hurried to the fly and asked, "Yes, sir?"

"Faulkner, get word to Captain Piper. I want a half troop of his light horse ready to ride in twenty minutes. Twenty minutes, do you understand?" He thought a minute. "Tell Piper not to delay for provisions or anything else except to make sure his men have full pouches of ammunition." He paused and thought a moment. "Tell him I'll have a column following him to provide support and they'll be carrying oats for his horses and provisions for his men."

Faulkner saluted. "Yes, sir. I'll send a messenger right away."

"No messenger, Faulkner. Go yourself; tell Piper that Joshua Baird will be riding with them and he'll explain what it's all about. Now get going, sir! Twenty minutes, do you understand?"

Bouquet turned back to Baird. "Joshua, ride down that train and get the munitions. Capture the men — that's important. If we can get them, we'll have the evidence we need to put that gentleman you and I discussed out of business for good."

Baird smiled broadly and said, "Yes, sir!"

Bouquet looked at Stirling. "Captain, you'll command the support column. Take your company and McDonald's. They're both full of men who fought at Bushy Run and they know how to handle themselves in the forest. You heard what I said about carrying supplies for Piper's horses and men, so get some pack horses loaded with what's required. It shouldn't be much; I don't expect this little expedition last beyond tomorrow afternoon at the latest. So get on the trail as fast as you can."

"Yes, Colonel; you'll hear the drums beating assembly as soon as I can get back to our camp line." He saluted and turned to leave.

Welford was still standing in the entrance to the tent, a bemused expression on his face at how rapidly things had changed.

Bouquet glanced at his former adjutant and then grinned. "And Thomas," Bouquet called to Stirling, "Be sure Mr. Welford goes with you. It's time he sees some action."

Welford looked startled at the colonel's words.

Bouquet looked at Welford. "What are you standing there for, Lieutenant? Shouldn't you be going to get your kit and then muster your men?"

Welford gulped, saluted, and then he, too, left.

Joshua pointed at Welford and said, "That bastard shot my horse out of hand, Colonel. The animal would have been fine with a little doctoring. The man's lucky I didn't kill him right on the spot. I'm goin' to be plain with you, sir; he don't belong out here on the border."

"He does try my patience, Joshua. But I'm giving him a chance. And frankly, he does have his uses back in Philadelphia and New York."

Baird shrugged and said, "I'll be on my way, Colonel. I've got to get another horse." He took Mary by the arm and started to leave.

Bouquet held up his hand. "Not so fast, Joshua; we still some have some business."

"What do you mean, sir? The light horse will be ready to go soon."

"Joshua, I'm sure you had a good reason for being outside the lines with this young lady. And for providing information to a band of Mingoes who are still our enemy. Now is the time to give me an explanation."

Joshua started to respond, but Mary interrupted him. "Sir, it's all my doing. A white woman living with the Mingo, named Abigail Gibson, came to me asking for medical information. She acts as doctor to many villages. She . . ."

Bouquet held up his hand. "I was quite familiar with Miss Gibson before she was captured. And I have been apprised of her current medical role among the Mingo. Just tell me on what grounds you felt it necessary to provide her with medical information."

"She wanted to be able to perform smallpox inoculations among her people. She's afraid of a big epidemic after all the contact with Europeans during this campaign." Mary thought for a minute, searching for a way to put her actions in as favorable a light as possible. "And there are a lot of white hostages among the Indians. I thought it would help them as well as the Indians if I gave her the information on how to make the inoculations."

Bouquet crossed his arms. "So you are telling me that you took it upon yourself to provide this information without consulting the surgeon or any other officer?" He looked at Joshua and continued, "And you agreed to help her? After working with the army all these years? Surely you both knew that you were providing comfort to an enemy of the crown?"

Mary said, "Sir, as I said, I thought it would help white hostages."

Bouquet stamped his foot. "Miss Fraser, one of our primary demands to the tribes is that they turn over their hostages. That is the real help they need. Your intentions are quite misguided."

"But sir, everybody knows that they won't turn over all of them. And the reason that I had to go outside the lines was because the Slippery Rock Creek Mingoes were going home to avoid giving up their hostages."

"That is no reason to provide assistance to them. In fact, their recalcitrance is firm grounds for treating them as hostiles! Now Miss Fraser, I am well aware of your service to the army; you performed commendably at Bushy Run and suffered a serious wound. But how can I excuse your actions in this case?"

Joshua burst out, "Oh, for God's sake, Henry, the truth is she was helping Abigail because she has a son by Wend Eckert. He's five years old. She wanted to make sure the little lad was protected against the smallpox. That's the long and the short of it."

Bouquet stood riveted in place as if struck by a bolt of lightning, his mouth wide open. Then he said, very slowly, "Young Eckert has a son by Abigail Gibson?"

Joshua nodded. "That be the truth of it, Colonel." He looked directly into Bouquet's eyes. "And, Henry, we both know damn well that ever since that massacre on Forbes Road, you've been lookin' after Wend as if he were the son you never had. Now are you goin' to punish the woman who had no idea 'cept to help his son?"

Bouquet spun on his heel so that his back was to them. He crossed his arms again and he stared into the distance. Mary could see muscles working in his face.

Joshua said quietly, "There be times to break the rules, Henry."

Bouquet spun around to face the pair. He looked at Mary. "And just what is your interest in Mr. Eckert and his child? I don't fathom why you would risk everything to help his child."

Mary looked down at the ground.

Baird said, "Henry, look at the girl and think about things like a man instead of a colonel."

Bouquet stared at Mary for a moment, and then he raised his eyebrows and nodded slowly. He sighed and said, "Ah, yes; I understand; you're in love with Eckert and would do anything you could do to help him or his offspring."

Mary looked up at Bouquet and felt tears rolling down her cheeks. "I'll na' deny it, Colonel."

Bouquet looked at Mary's face. "Miss Fraser, Captain McDonald always vowed that you were a proper soldier." He reached into his pocket and pulled out a handkerchief and handed it to her. Then he said softly, "Proper soldiers don't cry."

Joshua walked over and stood beside Mary, putting his hand on her shoulder. "You got to consider, Henry, that if we capture this pack train and bring the Shawnee to terms, it all started with Mary here."

Bouquet set his jaw. "I will have to take all this into consideration. And I make no promises. But now is the time for action. Joshua, get mounted and join Piper." He pointed at Mary. "And you, Miss Fraser, return to your duty and do me the courtesy of staying out of trouble."

* * *

Mary walked back to the hospital amidst a camp abuzz with preparations. The half troop of cavalrymen were standing-to with their mounts in hand. In the distance she saw Baird saddling a fresh horse while he talked to Captain Piper. Other soldiers were standing in groups watching the activity in the cavalry camp, shouting jests at the horseman. Meanwhile, the insistent beat of drums was summoning the men of Stirling's and McDonald's companies to assemble. In the distance she could see packhorse men loading six animals with provisions. Troops from all the battalions were gathered in their camp lines, speculating at the cause of all the sudden action.

Just as she arrived at the hospital, Mary heard the brassy sound of a hunting horn and turned to see the light horsemen, with Joshua and Piper at the head of the column, heading for the northern lines of the camp.

Kathryn and the two orderlies were standing together watching the departure of the horse troop. Taggart said in a sarcastic tone, "Well Mary, I'm gratified you finally made it back. You were supposed to be here an hour ago."

Kathryn was staring at Mary. "Taggart, her bein' late is 'na the real problem. Look at her face! It's all cut and bruised. What happened, lass?"

"It's a long story Kathryn. I got it by falling off a horse."

"Well, let's get you cleaned up. Come over to the treatment tent where I can clean out all those scratches."

Taggart and Lister followed behind, and stood watching while Kathryn worked on Mary. Taggart asked, "And just what were you doing on a horse, Mary?"

Mary sighed. She realized that events were going to bring out her story in very short order. It would be better to tell her comrades directly instead of letting them get it through camp rumors. So she gave them a summary of the day's events.

Kathryn shook her head. "Then you're responsible for all the commotion goin' on in the camp?"

Mary sighed. "Yes, I'm afraid so."

Taggart said, "Good Lord, lass. Are you on report for leaving the camp?"

"I don't know. I'm sure Bouquet will tell our colonel the whole story. I guess my fate will all be up to him; him and Munro."

Kathryn shook her head. "And Munro's already upset with you for showing that Mingo woman the medical book."

Mary nodded. "Yes, and there's more I'm going to have to tell him when he gets back."

Suddenly a sharp voice came from behind the little group. "Then you had better start telling me now."

Mary looked up to see Surgeon Munro standing behind Taggart and Lister. He had his hands on his hips and was obviously harboring a smoldering anger. Beside him, his hands in his pockets, was Doctor Highsmith. Mary could find no words and simply looked down at the table.

Munro said, "Miss Fraser, when Kathryn finishes tending your wounds, you will report to my tent and we shall discuss your outlandish behavior today." He turned on his heel and left, followed by his provincial counterpart.

Kathryn whispered, "You're in for it now, lass. I never saw the surgeon with so much anger in his eyes. God, I hope he don't throw you out of the hospital."

In a few minutes, with great trepidation in her heart, Mary came to the flap of Munro's tent. Physically, she felt miserable; her cheek was still stinging and her right leg and shoulder had begun to throb from the delayed effect of the fall. She looked into the tent; Munro was seated at his writing table, a scowl on his face, and Highsmith was leaning against the rear tent pole, drawing on his pipe. His face was emotionless.

Mary entered and stood in front of the table.

Munro shook his head. "I do not know what has possessed you, Mary Fraser. I've known you for a long time and until the last few days you've never acted irresponsibly." He paused. "I've just been told by Colonel Reid about your escapade outside of our lines. He learned of it from Bouquet himself. I don't know all the details, but what you did was a clear violation of posted orders and an act of willful involvement with the enemy."

Mary took a deep breath. "Am I under charges, then Mr. Munro?"

Munro stared at her for a long time without responding, his jaw set and the muscles of his face working. Then he shook his head and said, "Not at present. For some reason — which I vow is beyond my ability to fathom — Bouquet asked Colonel Reid to suspend action against you for the time being."

Mary sighed in relief. *Maybe I'm in purgatory, not hell.*

Munro pounded the table. "But that does not mean you won't answer to *me* right now. The fact is, I gave you precise orders to avoid contact with the Mingo. And you certainly understood that you were on probation here in the hospital. Instead of taking that to heart, you deliberately set out to meet with that Mingo hostage woman again."

Mary felt herself shaking. "Yes, I admit that. And I must confess to something else, Mr. Munro." She pointed to the surgeon's medical reference. "I cut the pages on smallpox out of that book and gave them to her."

"What!" Munro turned and picked up the book. He quickly flipped through the pages until he came to the missing sheets. "By God, Miss Fraser, do you understand what you've done? You have mutilated crown property! Besides disobeying my express orders, you're a thief!"

"I'm sorry, Mr. Munro. It was just that I felt great sympathy for that woman and her son. I know it won't excuse my actions, but the boy is Eckert's son and I felt compelled to help him."

A look of surprise came over Highsmith's face. He pushed himself away from the tent post and took the pipe out of his mouth. "Eckert? Did I hear her say, *Eckert?* Is she referring to Mr. Wend Eckert, late of Sherman Valley?"

Munro looked over at Highsmith. He said impatiently, "Yes, yes; Wend Eckert; he was a scout during last year's expedition. It was well known that he and Mary carried on a youthful infatuation with each other all summer."

Highsmith's face wrinkled up into a broad smile and he laughed. "Now I'll be damned! That man does get around." Then he leaned back against the tent pole, still grinning to himself.

Mary exclaimed, "It wasn't a childish infatuation, Mr. Munro. It was the genuine love of two people old enough to understand their own emotions. That's why I was so determined to help his son, even one by another woman."

Highsmith said quietly, "Mary, are you aware that Eckert has since married another woman?"

"Yes, Dr. Highsmith. He did that because he thought I was dead. But it's sure he would have married me if he'd known the truth. Joshua Baird told me that."

Munro pounded the table. "Enough talk of Eckert. I don't care what bloody emotions you let rule you, Mary. The fact is, you willfully violated my orders and damaged crown property. How can I ever trust you again? And if I can't trust you, how can I permit you to work for me here in the hospital?"

Mary felt panic. "Oh, no sir. Please, you can't send me away. Working here has been my life!"

Munro shook his head. "There's nothing for it, Mary. I'm going to Colonel Reid and tell him I can't have you in the hospital anymore."

Mary felt tears forming in her eyes. Her heart was racing. Then she heard Highsmith clear his throat.

"Percy, I think you're being a bit hasty. It does appear that the girl acted out of rash, youthful emotion, rather than any purposeful intent to hurt the crown or defy you." He stepped away from the tent post and tapped his pipe to empty the ash. "Besides, we're short-handed enough and we've got to be ready to look after all these hostages in a few days. And there's no doubt that besides being your best nurse, Miss Fraser can write and calculate the daily reports. In other words, she's more valuable to you than even Taggart and Lister. We'd be spiting ourselves if we sent her away."

Munro gritted his teeth. "Charles, she's openly defied authority. She must be punished."

"Indeed, Percy. But in punishing her, let's not punish ourselves. Besides, it seems even Bouquet is considering having some leniency with her." Highsmith picked up the medical book. "Tell you what, Percy; I have my own copy of this book. I'll give you my copy in exchange for yours; then you and the crown will be made whole."

Munro pointed to the book. "But then you, sir, shall be left with an incomplete reference."

"No I won't."

"How can that be?" Munro said in puzzlement.

"Because, Percy, as part of her punishment, Miss Fraser can spend her own time carefully copying, in her very fair hand, the missing pages onto paper so they can be inserted into my copy." He looked at Mary and then at Munro. "And of course, I'm sure Miss Fraser would benefit from some extra duties assigned by you to complete her punishment. I'll wager that performing additional work in the evening would give her time to reflect on the rashness of her recent actions."

Munro looked into the distance. Mary thought she could see his anger beginning to wane. She began to breathe easier and her heart slowed.

Munro drummed his fingers on the table. Much of the stress had drained out of his face. "Charles, I must admit that much of what you say is true. And working extra would indeed give her time to understand the gravity of her misdeeds." He turned to Mary and waved a finger at her. "But be aware, Miss Fraser, that this is your last chance. My patience with you is over. I'll have you out of here if there is any more insubordination. You'll be spending your time as a washerwoman. And the fact is you still may have to answer for all this with Colonels Reid and Bouquet."

* * *

"There! Did you hear it?" Kathryn was standing between two tents in the late afternoon sun, her hand cupped to her ear.

Mary asked, "Hear what?"

"I thought I heard gunfire; lots of it far in the distance."

Mary stood still and listened. "I don't hear . . ." But then she did; it was faint, almost sensed more than heard, but definitely there. "Yes, yes! Musket fire; I hear it!" She listened again and thought she heard a volley. "It's to the west!"

Others had heard it too, for a sudden quiet descended over the camp as people stopped what they were doing and froze in place, listening. With the camp background noise gone, the gunfire was more audible.

Kathryn almost whispered, "There it is again; its continuous now, as if the men are shooting on their own."

"Yes, it's pretty steady," said Mary.

Munro and Highsmith came out of their tent. Mary heard Munro say, "Stirling must be engaged. That's the firing of a lot of men, not a few light cavalry."

Highsmith nodded. "You're right. But I don't understand; supposedly they were going out after a few rogue traders. It must be they've encountered a force of Indians; nothing else would explain such a volume of fire."

Munro was about to say something, but his words stayed frozen in his mouth, for suddenly the sound of drums interrupted him. First it was a single drummer at headquarters, then drummers all over the camp took up the same beat. It was the unmistakable call to arms. Suddenly the camp came alive and there was a great clattering as soldiers put on their accouterments and grabbed their muskets. Then there was the sound of men running to their stations at the camp's barricades.

Munro shouted to his staff: "We need to get ready for casualties. If Piper and Stirling are heavily engaged, there will be work for us. Break out all the equipment and supplies. Get set up for operating!"

As they made their preparations, they watched the actions of the soldiers in the camp. With Stirling's and McDonald's companies absent, Bouquet ordered the grenadier company of the 60th up to the barricades to fill in and ordered other companies to extend their lines to further cover the gap.

Shortly the adjutant, Lieutenant Faulkner, came riding along the lines, providing information and orders to captains of the various companies. As he passed the hospital, Munro waved him down. "What's happening, Lieutenant?"

Faulkner leaned down from his horse. "We don't know any more than you do, Mr. Munro. Obviously Piper and Stirling have run into a fight with hostiles. Colonel Bouquet thinks its Shawnees from the west, but we can't ignore the possibility its actually parties of Indians from the camp right here. It could be that young warriors are revolting against the peace terms and are defying their chiefs."

Munro looked in the direction of the tribal camp. "That could upset everything."

Faulkner nodded. "True, sir. But all we can do now is take precautions in case there's an attack on our lines." He paused and waved toward the Indian camp. "The fact is we don't see any increase in activity among the Delawares and Mingoes in camp. Bouquet has sent some of the scouts over to the Indian village to talk with the chiefs and see what they say is going on."

Just then there was a loud explosion in the distance. The camp became deathly silent. Then Highsmith pointed to the west. "Damn, look, at that!"

His words were unnecessary, for all eyes were already looking in the direction of the noise. And now a pillar of black smoke was visible exactly where the sound of musketry had been coming from.

Highsmith said, "That could only be the gunpowder the traders were carrying. The question is: Did the traders blow it up to keep our men from getting it or did our men blow it to keep the hostiles from getting it?"

Falkner, still staring at the smoke, said, "Indeed, that's a good question, Doctor. But we won't know till we get word from the column." Then he turned his horse and continued down the line of barricades.

The staff of the hospital finished up their preparations. Meanwhile, the camp waited in tense expectation, still standing to arms. After about an hour, the word filtered down the line that the Indians in the encampment had remained peaceful. The chiefs of the various tribes had let Bouquet know that they had no part in whatever hostilities were occurring.

It was just near the end of dusk that a mounted courier rode into camp with a message for Bouquet. And a few minutes later the headquarters drums began beating the stand-down call. Not long afterwards, everyone heard the sound of drums and bagpipes approaching. Then, in the very last moments of light, the column began entering the camp.

In the rear of the formation Mary could make out a group of wounded, some walking, some on horseback, and some carried by others. As she watched, the wounded segment broke off and headed for the hospital.

All of the staff rushed to receive the casualties.

As Mary looked at the straggling group, she felt a tug at her heart. The leading man was Robert Kirkwood, his musket slung over his shoulder. She looked at him but could see no signs of injury. "Bob, are you all right?" she shouted.

"There's 'na a thing wrong with me, lass. There was nary a ball with my name on it today. The captain put me in charge of getting all these men back from the bush and into your hospital." He turned to Munro. "Mr. Munro, I'm reporting to you with seven wounded; four walkin' mostly on their own power and three up on horses." Then he motioned to the very rear of his detachment. "And on that last string of horses are some men who'll be needin' only the gravedigger."

Munro called to his staff: "Let's get them all on blankets in the tents." He turned to Kirkwood. "Corporal, I'll ask you to have your squad help our staff with the wounded who can't walk. And lay out the dead behind the tent line for now."

Kirkwood nodded. "Yes, Surgeon, we'll help as long as you need us. And then we're to report back to our company." As he walked past Mary he paused and said quietly, "Lass, take notice of the private sittin' on the third horse. I know you'll be wantin' to pay him some special attention."

Mary looked at the wounded man. His face was stained from black powder and he was hunched over in the saddle, as if very weak. Suddenly she realized it was Tim McGregor. She gasped, "Is he bad?"

"Bad enough; he's got a ball high up in his right leg. I hope we got him back in time to save it." Kirkwood hesitated a moment longer. "And one of the others on horseback is your favorite lieutenant. He took two arrows, but I think only the one in his chest is serious."

Mary saw Welford; there was a private on either side, helping him to stay on the horse. His face was also covered by powder stains and his eyes seemed to be staring straight ahead into the distance as if he was not aware of his surroundings.

She ran over to McGregor and looked up at him. His eyes were closed as he slumped over the horse's neck. The highlander's face was sheet-white below the powder stains. Mary turned to Kirkwood. "He's lost a lot of blood. We've got to get him on a pallet in one of the tents fast so his wounds can be treated. Have a pair of your men follow me and I'll show you where to place him."

After they had moved all the casualties into tents, Mary carried a bucket of water and some cloths to the one where McGregor lay. She knelt beside the high-lander, who still had his eyes closed. She thought: *He looks much younger asleep, almost like a little boy in repose.* Succumbing to a surge of emotion, Mary leaned over and gave him a soft kiss on his cheek.

McGregor opened his eyes for the first time. He said in a weak voice, which was only a shadow of his normal one, "Ah, our first kiss, Mary Fraser. And it only took a savage's ball in my leg to earn it."

Mary sighed and shook her head. "Timothy McGregor, I'll admit you're a hard man for a girl not to like."

"Now my beautiful Mary, that's what I been tellin' you all the time." He smiled and then looked down toward his wound. "Now, lass, will you be lettin' me know if they'll be takin' my leg away from me?"

Mary reached down and raised McGregor's kilt. There was a tourniquet above the wound and a roughly applied bandage around his right thigh. Blood was oozing from the wound. She adjusted the tourniquet and was able to vir-tually stop the flow of blood. Then she untied the bandage and looked at the wound. It was a mess with both fresh and dried blood obscuring it. "I'll need to clean it up before I can say anything." She dipped a cloth into the bucket and then sponged the wound out. When she was done, she held a candle lantern close to the bullet hole. "It's in the fleshy part of your thigh, Tim. That's good, but the ball is still in there. I think it must have been mostly spent when it hit you, or it would have gone right through. But here's the good news: It didn't hit any bone."

"Now thank the Lord for all of that." McGregor smiled again and this time there was the old twinkle in his eyes. "Now aside from that wound, lass, do you be likin' what you see down there?"

Mary gave him a hard glance, although inside she felt like giggling. She said firmly, "In six years of nursing, Private McGregor, I've seen the parts of many a man in both the 77th and the 42nd. Don't you be going around thinking you have anything special."

She got up and looked down at McGregor. "You'll be all right until the doc-tor sees you. I have to look in at some of the others now."

105

Mary continued her rounds and entered the tent where Welford, as the only officer, lay by himself. Mary asked, "How are you doing, sir?"

The lieutenant didn't answer; he simply lay on his blanket, staring upward.

Mary said, "I'm here to clean you up, sir. The doctor is going to treat your injuries as soon as he finishes with the lightly wounded men."

This time Welford seemed to hear her for the first time; he turned his head to look at Mary. Suddenly his eyes opened wide in apparent fear. "You!" he said in a strained voice; then he just seemed to retreat back into himself and resume his long-distance stare.

Mary worked quickly to clean up the officer. He had arrowheads in his left calf and his left chest; in each case someone had broken off the shaft a couple of inches above the skin. Mary folded up a blanket and placed it under his leg to take the pressure off of the calf injury. The wounds were serious, but Mary was surprised how disoriented Welford was; she had seen men who were much more seriously injured who still kept all their wits about them.

Through it all Welford continued to passively stare at the top of the tent. She quietly got up and backed out through the flap.

She nearly bumped into Kirkwood, who was standing in the corridor between tent rows

"Now how are you bearing up, lass?"

Mary sighed. "I'm fine, Bob. But we're going to be working for a long time with this lot." She looked up to the treatment tents and saw Munro had one of the men who had arrived on horseback on the operating table, working to extract a bullet in his arm. Taggart and Kathryn were assisting him. The scene was illuminated by the light of several candle lanterns. Beyond the tent, Doctor Highsmith and Lister worked on one of the walking wounded in front of the fire. Mary turned back to Kirkwood. "What happened out there, Bob?"

Kirkwood shrugged. "Piper overtook the pack train way before he expected; the traders had gone into camp, just seven or eight miles to the west of here. The pack horses had been unloaded and the powder kegs and other goods was stacked up like they was getting ready for trading. The bastards heard the sound of the light horse coming and took off into the bush. Before running, they stampeded the pack horses to make things more confusing. Baird and some of the light horse tried to track down the traders, but what with the horses moving around in the bush and the head start the rogues had got, they couldn't find any of them."

Mary sighed and shook her head. "That's bad news. Bouquet wanted to capture some of the traders for evidence against their leader." Then she asked, "What brought on the fight? We heard lots of musketry."

"Stirling and McDonald and Piper were standing around trying to figure out how to get all them trading goods back when we was hit by the Indians." Kirkwood shook his head. "There must have been several war parties, 'cause they attacked from both the west and north. The first we knew, there was a cloud of arrows just comin' out of the bush, silent like." He motioned toward the tent behind Mary. "Welford got hit right away; he was with his half-company which had set up positons to the west. First he took an arrow in his leg and then a second later the one in his chest. He just dropped to the ground. Stirling saw what was going on and shouted, 'To trees!' We all took cover and the shootin' became fierce."

Mary asked, "Is that when these men got wounded?"

"Some of them was hit in that first surprise and in the shooting between us and the hostiles that happened right after that. But after a while, Stirling organized a charge; a charge on two fronts. He fixed bayonets and attacked to the westward with his company and part of McDonald's — that's where most of the enemy were skulking. At the same time, McDonald attacked to the north with a half-company where there was another group of hostiles firing. That chased them away, but more of the lads were hit. So we pulled back and took up positions around the trade goods. Everyone expected the savages to come back from another direction, just like they did that first day at Bushy Run. But they just disappeared into the bush and kept going."

"When was Timothy hit?"

"Ah, lass, I got to tell ya', the laddie was brave. You got to be proud of him. He was one of the first men who were up and at the Indians when Stirling called for the charge. He surprised a warrior and took the bastard down with his bayonet; he had just finished the Indian when he was hit with a ball. He lay there by the dead savage, 'na screamin' or saying anything. After things quieted, I put a tourniquet around his leg with my own hands and then Tavish and me carried him back into the middle of the position."

Mary nodded. "I knew Tim would do well." Then she thought of something. "Bob, why is Welford so fearful? He looks like he saw a ghost."

Kirkwood put his head back and laughed. "He's like that because Joshua put the fear of God into him."

"What do you mean, Bob?"

"Well, where Welford was laying was out in the bush, all alone after the charge was over. So, when we had finished moving McGregor, Tavish and I went back to get Welford." Kirkwood looked at Mary and grinned broadly. "But Baird had already got there. He was kneeling beside the lieutenant, with a pistol to the side of his head, pointed right at his ear. Tavish and I stood there watching." He shook his head. "Joshua was leaning over him and had this fierce, devilish look on his face like I 'na saw before. He said to Welford, 'I've been fightin' on the border all my life, Lieutenant. I know when a man is too bad hurt to be moved. So I'm going to put you down, just like you did to my horse'. Welford shouted, 'No! No, Baird! For God's sake don't shoot'." Kirkwood grinned. "Then Joshua said, 'Here it comes, Welford' and pulled the trigger on the pistol. Welford heard it click and starting squealing; squealing like a stabbed pig."

Mary was confused. "The gun didn't go off? Did it misfire?"

"Naw, lass. That was the joke on Welford. Joshua had blown all the powder from the pan. He just wanted to scare the shit right out of that dandy. And it's sure he did that."

Mary laughed. "Then what happened?"

"Welford screamed at Tavish and me. He said, 'You saw it! You saw what that man did. You're witnesses! I'll have you up on charges, Baird! You'll feel the lash!'."

Kirkwood grinned and said, "But then I answered up, 'I think those wounds have got you confused, Lieutenant; I didn't see nothing; not a thing 'cept him trying to help you,' and Tavish laughed and said, 'All I saw was Baird lookin' at your wounds to see how bad you were, and that's what I'll swear to the captain.' So then Baird put his pistol back into his belt and said, 'Take him back to the lines, lads'." Kirkwood waved at the tent again. "And Welford ain't said another word since; just stares off into the distance like you see him now."

Mary asked, "What about the explosion? It felt like the earth was shaking. How did that happen?"

"After the attack, Stirling, Piper, and McDonald got together. Stirling didn't like being isolated in the bush, not knowing how many Indians was around and whether they might attack. So he decided to get back to the camp as soon as possible. Since the pack horses had been set loose and were all over the bush, the officers decided there weren't no choice but to destroy the trade goods. So they loaded one horse with samples of all the goods and had us pile up the rest. Then we marched off; Piper and some of his men stayed behind to blow the powder."

Then Mary thought of something else, and asked, "What kind of Indians were they, Bob? Were they Shawnees who attacked you?"

Kirkwood shrugged. "All I know is that they were the kind of Indians who shot arrows and musket balls at us, lass. Maybe Joshua or the officers know who they were." Then he reached over and picked up his musket from where it leaned against a tent pole. "I'll say good night to you now, Mary. I got to get my lads and report back to Captain Stirling."

CHAPTER EIGHT
Days of Uncertainty

An exhausted Mary Fraser sat in front of the fire, a blanket over her shoulders, absorbing the heat from the flames and the gentle warmth of the early morning sunlight. She held a large mug of tea in her hands, savoring the taste of it. As she sipped the liquid, she reflected on the events of the last twelve hours. The hospital staff had worked through the night tending wounds and ensuring the comfort of the injured soldiers. It had taken a long time to deal with the three seriously wounded men.

Highsmith, Mary, and Lister had spent much of the night working on Welford's wounds. The arrowhead in his leg had come out without much problem and without significant damage to the calf muscles. But the chest wound was another matter. The arrowhead was deeply embedded in flesh and muscles. There was no way it could simply be backed out like they had done with the calf wound yet it was not deep enough to try pushing it through his body. Instead Highsmith had to delicately probe around and do some judicious cutting to free the rear barbs of the brass head and then slowly work it free.

As she watched, Mary gained a great appreciation for the Pennsylvania surgeon's skill. Highsmith had a delicate touch and great patience. She had given Welford a copious amount of rum to sedate him and then worked with Lister to restrain the officer at the most painful moments of the procedure. But Welford earned a degree of her respect, for he gritted his teeth on a leather strip and bore the pain manfully and was able to hold himself still under the knife with little help from Mary and the orderly. Fortunately for the lieutenant, just as they were about to finally withdraw the arrowhead, he lost consciousness and was spared the most painful part of the operation. Now he was resting peacefully in the tent.

Munro, Kathryn, and Taggart had worked on the other two seriously wounded. They had had to take the lower arm of one man, named Peter McWhorter; his forearm bones had been literally shattered by a ball. But Mary's assessment about

Tim McGregor had been correct; the ball in his thigh was extracted with relative ease and the bleeding was controlled with no trouble. Munro was confident that he would regain the complete use of his leg.

Mary's thoughts were interrupted when she looked up to see Ian Tavish walking toward her. The piper was loaded with personal gear; a pack, haversack, and a leather pouch.

He stopped in front of the fire. "Good morning to you, Mary." He shook his head. "I'd 'na be lyin' to say you're looking a little worn down at this moment."

Mary answered, "And you'd be right. We've been busy tending the wounded men. I'm ready for bed, but I don't know when I'll be able to go to my blankets. The morning chores have to be finished."

Tavish held up the items he was carrying. "Kirkwood asked me to bring over Tim McGregor's kit. It seems he'll be spending some time with you."

Mary sighed and patted the ground beside her. "He's asleep; drop his stuff here. I'll take it to him when I've finished my tea." As Tavish deposited the gear, Mary looked up and asked, "Where's Joshua? I haven't seen him since he left with Piper's Horse yesterday."

"Ah, now Mary, you'll 'na be seeing him for a while. He rode out with three other scouts this mornin'. They're lookin' to see what's going on to the west after that fight yesterday." Then he nodded in the direction of the patient tents. "Take good care of Tim; he's been a boon to Stirling's company and he handled himself damn well yesterday, even after the wound."

"So Kirkwood told me. Of course I'll take good care of him."

"You know he's got a powerful likin' for you, Mary, and you could do a lot worse than to marry a man like that."

"Tavish, if I was looking to get married, why would I take a private when there are corporals and sergeants coming around to keep me company?"

"You're a hard one for being so young, Mary Fraser."

"Tavish, you know very well I've been with the army since the 77th was raised in '56. That's nine years out of my sixteen. Sure and I've learned enough not to marry a new private who barely gets enough of the king's coin to keep himself, let alone keep a wife." She hesitated a moment and said, "Now go back to your company, Tavish. I don't want to discuss Timothy McGregor any more. And you can tell Captain Stirling that the private is keeping his leg and will be back in the ranks in good time."

The piper gave Mary a crooked smile, nodded to himself, and then said, "I'm thinkin' you're 'na so hard as you're tryin' to make out, Mary. I think you're more stuck on the lad than you admit." With that, he turned and strode off back toward the camp of the 42nd.

As she watched him go, Mary felt a flash of anger at the piper for his last comment. She took a sip of the tea and in a few seconds her temper cooled as rapidly as it had flared. The source of her agitation was, of course, the fact Tavish was right; she was falling in love with the brash, constantly cheerful, and yes, handsome young highlander. For the first time since her days with Wend, she was feeling a serious emotional and physical attraction for a man. But every time she thought about McGregor, she also had a sense that she was betraying the memory of Wend Eckert. Mary thought to herself: *Why should I feel guilty about loving another man when Wend is married and about to have another child?*

She sighed. There was simply no good reason; *none at all.* She had told Joshua she would deal with her feelings for Wend. *It was time she started doing it.*

Mary gulped the last of the tea, pushed herself to her feet, and started off to face her morning chores.

* * *

Mary finally got several hours of sleep in the middle of the day. Her exhaustion was such that even the loud bustle of the camp around her did not intrude on her slumber. That was a rare occurrence, for she was normally a light, fitful sleeper.

Kathryn finally woke her up in the late afternoon. "It's time for evening chores, Mary. And we got to tend all these wounded."

"All right, all right; I'm awake." She sat up. "How are the wounded doing? Are there any problems? Is Tim all right?"

"They're all doing as well as could be expected. And you can look in on that devil McGregor for yourself." Kathryn looked up the tent row. "You take Tim and Welford, and I'll look in on McWhorter to see how his stump is doing. And I'll take the walking wounded; they're all in one tent."

Mary decided to get the distasteful part of her work over first, so she started with Welford. She entered his tent to find that he was awake and had emerged from the stupor which had affected him the previous night. She put down her bucket and supplies. "I'm here to clean your wounds, Mr. Welford."

Welford stared at her. Then he said directly, "Your name's Mary Fraser."

"Yes, Lieutenant; that's correct." Mary quickly took the bandage and dressing off of the officer's leg and checked the condition of the wound and the stiches. "There's no sign of mortification there, sir.' She started to wash the injury.

Welford said peremptorily, "I know about you, Miss Fraser. The men of the company told me your story. It seems you are an orphan and the pet of the regiment; every man's little sister. They all smile when they talk about you."

"There's some who say that, sir. It is true that I've grown up in the 77th and 42nd. I know most of the men who came over with the 77th or who marched in both regiments with Bouquet last summer. I don't know many of the men from the new draft."

Mary finished with the leg wound and moved to the chest injury. She sat Welford up and propped him in that position with folded blankets. Then she unwound the bandage to look at the wound itself.

As she worked, her head just a foot or two from his, Welford spoke out in an imperious tone, "I've also learned about your *cherished* plan to become a governess."

Mary was startled by his words. She shot back, "Now how did you hear of that?"

"I was talking with the chaplain and Captain McDonald in the mess. They told me about your desire to leave the army and take service with a family of substance." Then he added, in a haughty voice, "Of course, your idea is a mere fantasy."

Mary stopped and looked him in the eye. "Why would you say that, Mr. Welford? I've studied hard and Chaplain MacLagen says I know more now than many tutors and governesses he has met." She thought a moment, then continued, "And I'm even learning French."

Welford laughed in her face. "It's not *what* you know, Miss Fraser; it's *who* you are. *Who* you are, do you understand? Upper class families want cultured young women from good families. The simple truth is that no wealthy family in England is going to engage someone like you — *a camp girl* from a marching regiment, for God's sake — to teach and nurture their children."

Mary felt a burst of anger and her face reddening. She stared at the lieutenant for a long time, fighting the urge to lash out at him. Finally, when she was under control, she said in measured tones, "Perhaps you're right about English gentry. But I'm sure there are many families in Scotland, in the lowlands or highlands, or perhaps here in the colonies, who would find my services worthwhile. And that's where I'll pursue employment."

"Ah, Miss Fraser; clearly you are a smart young lady, and," he looked her over, "Quite presentable in your own way. I do believe you'll find employment rather quickly if you leave the army. I should say you would do nicely as a *maid* in even the most exalted household."

Mary said nothing more; instead she simply finished putting Welford's dressing and bandage back on and left the tent.

She quickly walked around to the back of the tents, leaned up against a tree and crossed her arms. Welford's words had cut her to the quick and she felt moisture in her eyes. She knew the man was an ass, but she feared he was right. What he had said actually reflected her own deepest fears; she had long suspected that no respectable family would consider employing a girl of her background, whatever her level of learning and abilities.

Moreover, over the last few days she had seen all her cause for hope crumble before her eyes.

First the promise of Grenough's sponsorship had proven false and degrading.

Second, she was sure that her reputation among the officers of the regiment was tarnished by her actions of the last few days. Who among them would give her any kind of recommendation now, knowing the facts of her behavior? Undoubtedly they would all feel the same way about her as Munro. She sighed to herself. *What could she have been thinking to squander the good will and reputation she had built up over the years? She had let her emotions control her instead of sound logic from her brain.*

The fact was, at least in part because of her own foolishness, all that was left to her was the life of the regiment.

The reality of it all crashed down over her like someone had doused her with a bucket of cold water: *Her dream, the dream which had sustained her for years, was over.* Overwhelmed, Mary suddenly felt tears running down her cheeks. But she refused to let herself give way to sobbing. She set her jaw and wiped her eyes and face. Then she pushed herself away from the tree; there were wounded waiting and work to be done.

* * *

Late the next evening Mary stood by the fire, stirring a pot of stew which would be the supper for the hospital staff and their patients. The two doctors were at their respective messes. She looked up to see Baird come out of the darkness.

"Hello, lass!" There was a smile on his face and a cheerful lilt to his voice. In his hand was a small jug.

"Joshua, you're back! I had heard you were out for a long scout to the west."

"That was the plan, but it turned out there was no need for it." He held up the jug. "Let's have some cheer. I got this from your favorite camp woman, Laurie McPhie."

"I could have gone all day without hearing that woman's name. And I'll wager that jug cost you dear."

"Now, now, Mary, out here on campaign you have to find your drink where you can." He winked at her. "And the fact is that woman does have some fine assets."

Mary shook her head. "And she knows how to use every one of them for profit."

Baird grinned. "That she does. But let's sit by the fire and I'll give you the lay of the land."

They settled on a log, side by side. Joshua pulled the cork on the jug. The smell of rum rose from the opening. "It's been two days since I had a good pull and I vow I've never been more in need of it." He offered the vessel to Mary; she took a small sip, then handed it back to Baird.

She said, "We're treating seven wounded men from the fight. They buried several dead men yesterday." She looked up at Baird. "I've heard only bits and pieces of what happened out there. Tell me the whole story."

Joshua shook his head. "Things don't never go the way you expect in this business. I had it figured that Grenough's men were headin' west, fast as the pack horses could be driven, for the Shawnee villages on the Scioto. So Piper and I calculated we'd have to press hard for several hours to overtake the train, given the lead they had. But we was wrong; dead wrong. It turned out they was planning to meet with several bands of Indians right near here. So we was startled when we came upon their camp." He looked at Mary. "Surprised the hell out of me."

Mary said, "Kirkwood told me the traders heard you coming and ran away into the bush."

"Yeah, and they kept their wits about them. They took the time to stampede their pack horses before they took to their own mounts. So there was confusion all over the place. I lit out after them with a couple of Piper's boys, tryin' to catch at least one to take back to Bouquet like we planned. I was out for more'n two hours, but didn't have no luck. They split up and was movin' fast; all the tracks from them loose pack horses made it near impossible to pick up the right trail. So I finally rode on back to the place where they'd dropped the trade goods and Stirling's column was just commin' up when I got there."

"We heard a lot of shooting. Was it Shawnee's who attacked you?"

114

"Damn right. They hit us while Piper, Stirling, McDonald and me was standin' lookin at the pile of trade goods and tryin' to decide what to do. Before we knew it, we was hit by a quick volley of arrows and then musket fire. So Stirling had everyone take cover and fire back; firing was pretty fierce for a while and, I got to tell you, it looked like the Indians might roll over us. But Stirling and McDonald know their business damn well. Soon as they could they organized a bayonet charge and drove the savages away."

Joshua took a long pull on the jug. "I told Stirling that the Indians would be back and to get his men organized to receive another attack, probably from another direction. But damned if I wasn't wrong; wrong for the second time in one day." He shook his head. "Can you believe that? Anyway, we waited and waited, but there wasn't no new attack. So I went out and found them Shawnee's was all gone."

"Why do you think that happened, Joshua?"

"I found out, sure enough; them Shawnees was in such a hurry they missed carrying off one dead warrior. He was layin' right by your new love, that fellow McGregor."

"For God's sake, Joshua, he's not my new love. He's just a nice lad that I let visit with me."

"Well, he's a handsome devil; he should be your new love." Joshua grinned at her, then continued, "Anyway, I examined the corpse. That's how I was certain it was Shawnees. And then it didn't take long to figure out why they didn't keep attacking. I drained that dead warrior's powder horn; it were near empty. There weren't enough powder for but two or maybe three more shots."

"So they were desperately short on ammunition?"

"That's it exactly, lass. Then I looked around and found horse tracks; the Shawnee's had heavily laden packhorses with them. They was carrying pelts to do some big tradin'. The truth be they was as surprised as we was; runnin' into troops was the last thing they expected."

"That's what I don't understand, Joshua; why would the Shawnee's want to do their trading so close to the military camp here? There was a much better chance of it being detected than if they'd gone further west."

"That's a good question and exactly the one I had after we chased them Indians off. I had some hunches and naturally the name Charlot Kaske kept runnin' through my mind. But I still couldn't get it straight why they was tradin' here instead of over on the Scioto."

The scout took another long pull on the jug and wiped his mouth. Then he continued, "After lookin' over the dead Shawnee, I went back and joined the officers. They was tryin' to decide what to do about all the powder and other supplies. There wasn't enough packhorses or saddles still around to carry it back. Plus we had to use the horses we had to carry the wounded. And Stirling wasn't interested in stayin' out in the bush in the night to wait for more horses from the camp, not knowin' if another attack might happen. So we decided to take one horse-load of powder and other goods back as evidence and blow the rest."

Mary asked, "What did Bouquet say about all this?"

"He was pretty happy 'cause what we'd found out confirmed that the Shawnee's was really short of war provisions. But he was disappointed we hadn't been able to capture any of the traders. I looked over the powder kegs and blades; them traders was smart about that, too. There weren't any markings to show where they had come from."

"Isn't there anything Bouquet can do about Grenough legally? For God's sake, there must be something!"

Joshua shook his head. "It don't look good. Henry and I talked that over for a while. There's still no real solid evidence. It looks like all he'll be able to do is cut Grenough out of any more contracts with the army."

Mary set her jaw. "So the fact is, Grenough won't be punished."

Baird sighed. "Maybe not in a legal way; but remember, that bastard did just lose a lot of money invested in those war supplies that went up in smoke." He waved his finger. "And there's more; Grenough has had a bad couple of years. In June of '63, just before Bouquet marched to Pitt against the tribes, Wend and me destroyed a pack train of powder Grenough's men was tradin' with Delawares out on Sideling Hill; then last December, when we was on Stirling's mission into the Ohio Country, we shot two of his men tradin' on the banks of the Allegheny; the Indians got all that powder, guns, and lead and were able to keep their pelts. Finally, there was that great wagon load of his supplies that Wend burned back in June in the Tuscarora Mountains. Think on it lass: Grenough has lost four loads of goods in a short time and got nothing in return. He's got to be feelin' the hurt in his pocket pretty bad."

Mary thought for a moment. "But now that the Indians have agreed to peace, trading with them will become legal again. And he told me he was planning to set up stores in settlements along Forbes Road. Now that the war is over, there will be lots of settlers moving westward." Mary looked at Joshua. "The truth is, it may take a while but Grenough will be able to recoup his fortunes."

Joshua shrugged and then said, "Yeah, Richard has always been able to land on his feet, no matter what happens."

There was a long moment of silence between them. Finally, Joshua contin-ued, "Anyway, after we finished talking about Grenough, Bouquet told me to get a group of scouts and range out to the west; he wanted me to see what the Shawnees were up to after losing all them supplies."

Mary stood up, stirred the pot, and threw some wood onto the fire. "You said at the beginning you didn't have to go far to find what you were looking for."

"Yeah, we rode down the westbound trail 'till evening; we made camp about twenty miles out. And we was just sittin' down to eat when a party of Shawnee's approached us."

"They just walked into your camp?"

Joshua nodded. "More or less; they was led by a man named Running Fox; some sort of minor leader. He said they came in peace and was carrying a mes-sage for Bouquet from the Shawnee chiefs. They had gotten together and decided to negotiate. Cornstalk is sending a chief named Red Hawk to represent all the Scioto villages. And he's bringing a number of white hostages to show their good faith. We sat at the fire and gossiped, and some rum was passed around, and the couriers started talking about what happened at Stirling's little skirmish." Baird grinned. "They said that it was Kaske, just like we figured, who had made arrangements to trade for the powder. And that it had been him and his followers who rounded up the pelts and went to meet Grenough's men."

Mary asked quickly, "Did they say why he set up the trading so near here?"

"Sure enough. He did it 'cause he thought if the Delawares and Mingoes saw he had lots of powder and lead, they might be convinced to join him on the warpath and that would mean the Shawnee chiefs would have no choice but to join in."

Mary shook her head. "He sure had big plans."

"Yeah, but the fact is, the explosion of that powder blowed away Kaske's influ-ence." Joshua squeezed Mary's arm. "And it turns out that the man your friend McGregor killed was Kaske's main lieutenant; the couriers said that when he was killed, the fight went out of the other warriors."

"So are you saying that Tim played a big role in turning the tide of the skirmish?"

"That the truth of it, if those Shawnee couriers are to be believed."

Mary said nothing, but looked into the fire. She felt a surge of admiration for the brash young private.

Joshua continued, "After the skirmish, most of the warriors who had been following Kaske knew it was all over and went back to their villages."

"So do you think the Shawnee chiefs are going to agree to Bouquet's conditions?"

"Yes, I think they'll be some dickering; the chiefs have to make it look like they ain't just plain surrendering. But they'll come around after a few days. They ain't got no choice."

"And what happened to Charlot Kaske himself?" Mary looked at Joshua. "Will he be coming to the negotiations?"

Joshua laughed. "Not a chance, lass. The word is that Kaske is holding out to the bitter end. There be only a handful of his closest warriors still following him. But he can't get himself to understand that the French are totally out of the game; so the couriers say he is taking what's left of his band and traveling west to see the French at Fort Chartres; it's on a river they call the Mississippi. That's where the Ohio ends up. Anyway, Chartres is the last garrison of French soldiers north of Louisiana. He's going to try to convince the commandant there to help him with ammunition so he can continue the war."

"My God, the fighting with the French has been over for four years. You don't think they'll actually help him?"

Joshua shook his head. "Naw, that's not in the cards; Kaske's just bitter, desperate, and too hard-headed to give up. I suspect that he may be doin' it just to save face. But that fort is hundreds of miles away and travlin' there will take him out of the picture for months."

Joshua took another gulp of the rum, then said, "This morning, we brought them Shawnee couriers back to camp to talk to Bouquet. They're going to stay as hostages 'till Red Hawk and his delegation arrive."

Mary bit her lip. "Joshua, now that things have worked out this way, what do you think that Colonel Bouquet will do about us going outside the lines to help Abigail? Munro expects that he or Colonel Field will have to punish me some way for violating orders." She paused a second, then asked, "Did you ask him about that?"

Then Mary sat down beside him and looked into the fire.

Baird filled his pipe and lit it with a burning stick from the fire. "Naw, he didn't say nothin' at all about it and I weren't about to rouse any sleeping dogs." Joshua shook his head, and put his arm around Mary. "Now don't you be worryin', girl. The colonel is so busy workin' things out with the Indians, he don't have no time to worry about somethin' so slight as that little rule breakin'."

Mary sighed. It was reassuring to hear Joshua say that, but she wasn't so sure he was right; it could be Joshua's third mistake in a row.

* * *

The next day saw the word spread through the camp about the arrival of the Shawnee couriers. By nightfall, there was universal optimism that the campaign would soon be over and peace obtained without any need for further combat. As night closed in, spontaneous celebration broke out in every unit. The hospital staff gathered at their campfire and, with great care, brought out the wounded to join them in the revelry. It was the first time that Tim McGregor had left his pallet; Mary propped him up next to the fire. Even McWhorter with his heavily bandaged stump was able to join the group. Kathryn's husband, Johnnie O'Hara came over from his company as did Kirkwood and Tavish. Welford, as an officer, remained behind in his tent in splendid solitude.

Kirkwood, in his role as quartermaster of Stirling's company, had managed to get his hands on some prime cuts of a recently slaughtered bullock, which they set to roasting on a spit over the fire. Taggart brought out his fiddle and played an assortment of spirited tunes which further brightened everyone's spirits.

Since her encounter with Welford in his tent, Mary had increasingly reconciled herself to the end of her dreams and the reality of the limited options for her life; staying with the army, which meant marriage, or seeking menial labor in the service of a family somewhere and eventual marriage to a man of her class. Now, as she sat among people who had been her friends all her life, sharing the comradeship of the night, the fire, the food and drink, she reflected that there were worse places she could end up. Her mind flew to the images of the squalor she had heard about in the streets of London and other cities in England. Maybe it was indeed time for her to simply accept her lot and make the most of it. She suddenly became aware of the beauty of the immediate world around her. She thought: *Here we are enjoying ourselves in a small island of activity and light, surrounded by a black ocean of wilderness, hundreds of miles from the mainland of settlement.* She looked up at the extraordinarily clear sky, alive with stars. *I have seen things and peoples few other girls of my age have seen or will see. Perhaps this is the life I was born to live.*

She was sitting beside Timothy McGregor. As if reading her thoughts, he turned to her and smiled. "It's a beautiful night in the midst of the forest, isn't it Mary?" He reached over and with a soft touch, took her hand in his.

Mary looked into his eyes, which were full of affection. Instead of pulling back her hand, which had been her first reaction, she closed her fingers around his and gave him a quick squeeze. And then she put her other hand on top of his and let it remain there and she leaned lightly against him.

For once, Timothy McGregor didn't have anything to say; he just looked down at Mary and smiled, his whole face wrinkling up into an expression of happiness.

A couple of hours later Surgeon Munro returned to the hospital. He stood before the group at the fire and everyone greeted him appropriately, the two orderlies standing up.

Munro nodded. "I'm glad everyone is having a good evening. And enjoy it as long as you like. However, I must tell you that tomorrow will be a busy day. I've just been informed that in the morning we will move the hospital over to the log cabins which have been built for the hostages. Colonel Bouquet believes we will conclude negotiations with the savages and start receiving the white prisoners in a day or two. And then we will have our work cut out for us."

He nodded again and then strode over to Welford's tent. They could hear him repeating the information to the lieutenant. Then they also heard him say, "By the way, Welford, Bouquet told me you'll be resuming duties on his staff as soon as we get back to Pitt. I trust that agrees with you." There was a mumbled reply which no one could make out. Then Munro went to his own tent and closed the flap.

Kirkwood grinned from ear to ear and whispered, "Now the lads in Stirling's company will be even merrier when I tell them that choice bit of news!"

Shortly after that the party around the fire broke up. Mary helped Tim back to his tent. For a moment they were alone and McGregor pulled her close, looked deeply into her eyes, and said, "Mary Fraser, you're the bonniest lass I've ever known. And I'm in love with you as any man can be with a woman." And then he pressed his lips against hers.

After the briefest of hesitation Mary kissed him back and put her arms around him tightly. They stood in embrace for a long moment, and then she pulled back. "It's time for you to take to your bed, Timothy." She helped him settle into his blankets, then turned to leave.

As she stood by the tent flap, he called out softly to her, "Mary, lass, you didn't say how you feel about me."

Mary laughed. "That kiss told you enough for now, Private McGregor. I have many things to think over. Just keep in mind that you're only the second man whose kiss I've returned like that." She smiled affectionately, "Now get some sleep."

CHAPTER NINE

The Beat of the Drums

The return of the white hostages from the Indians was an experience which remained etched in Mary's memory for the rest of her life. The process extended over several days as different tribal bands brought their captives to the log cabins for delivery to the hospital staff.

Mary witnessed scenes of incredible joy as wives, daughters, and sons were reunited with their fathers and brothers. There were many men, particularly in the Pennsylvania battalions, who had joined the expedition in the hope of recovering their lost family members. Every day they came to the cabin area to inspect the newly arrived captives and see if their relatives had at last been restored to them. Some found what they were looking for, others met nothing but disappointment.

But there was another side of the hostage return which opened Mary's eyes; that was the grief displayed by Indian men and women who turned over the captives. For it was soon clear to her that many of the hostages had strongly bonded with their captors and had become fully integrated with their woodland families. Mary had always thought of the Indians as stoic, solemn people with stone faces who shielded their emotions from view. Because of that, she was startled when she witnessed many warriors with their faces wrinkled up in grief and tears running down their cheeks. She saw Indian women parting with their adopted children with the same grief-stricken embraces of any white mother saying farewell to their natural born offspring. Many of the Indians returned to the cabin area to visit the hostages, bringing them baskets of their favorite food or gifts of warm clothing to wear on the trip back to the east.

Perhaps the greatest surprise to Mary was the number of hostages who were brought in bound with ropes because they were adamant in their desire to stay with their Indian families. These proved mostly to be young people or children who had been taken as infants or toddlers and had no conscious memory of the time they had spent with their white families. They had been raised as children of the forest, knew no other life, and found it impossible to understand why they must leave the only families they had ever known. Many wailed loudly in their tribal language not to be left behind when their adoptive parents finally departed. One cabin was set aside for these people and a guard posted at the door to prevent their escape.

Another cabin was dedicated as the nursery for the youngest children and Mary was put in charge of caring for them. She fed them and saw to their bathing; she did the best she could to entertain them, telling stories and helping them make up games. She was able to teach some of the youngsters who knew only Indian dialects a few words of English. It was very fulfilling to her, for it was the nearest thing to the kind of work she had hoped to spend her life performing.

Grown up returnees were allowed to roam the military camp, looking for friends or relatives. One of those who took advantage of that privilege was Simon Girty, the young Mingo hostage that Mary had talked to at the edge of the Indian camp. He had arrived in the first day of hostage returns. Mary was glad he liked to roam, for he seemed determined to befriend her. She made a point of being polite to him, but she was uncomfortable having him around. He was a little too brash and saucy for her liking. Then, on the third day of his freedom, Girty came back from a walk through the camp with information which Mary found extremely upsetting.

Mary was standing outside the nursery, leaning against the wall, taking a break from the constant attention required by the children. Girty walked up to her, a sly grin on his face.

"Well, Mary Fraser, I've been learning a lot about you around the camp," Girty positively leered at her. "All of it is very intriguing."

The facial expression and tone of his voice put Mary on her guard. "And what have you found out about me that's so interesting, Simon?"

"Ah now, since the day I first met you, I knew you were an independent and forward girl, but I didn't know how forward."

"Stop the taunting game, Simon. What have you learned that has you playing riddles with me?"

"I heard a story about how you were, uh, shall we say, *involved* with an important man named Grenough because you thought he could help you get ahead; he was going to help find you some comfortable position out of the army." He paused, then continued, "But then you had a falling out with him in his tent and slashed him in the face with a dagger, so bad that he had to leave the expedition." Girty grinned again. "Is that all true?"

Mary felt her face getting red. She tried to stay calm. "That's not the way it happened, Girty. And he didn't leave just because of the wound."

Girty laughed, then gave her a sly wink. "You don't have to be coy with me, Mary. It must have been disappointing for you; working so hard to cozy up to him and then losing out just 'cause you lost your temper."

"Girty, I don't know where you got this story from, but it's a lie; a wild perversion of the truth." She asked again, more insistently, "Who told you about this?"

"Lots of people know about it; but I got it first from a sassy looking woman name of *Laurie*, who was doing washing out behind the tents of Captain Graham's company."

Mary stamped her foot. "Oh, for God's sake; that's Laurie McPhie. She's the regimental gossip. Nobody believes what she says."

"Like I said, she wasn't the only one. And come on, you don't deny that you slashed him, do you? Lots of people saw the bandage on his cheek."

"No, that part is true, Simon."

"And it wouldn't be the first time that a pretty slip of a girl like you tried to use her charms to get what she wanted, would it?" He threw his head back and laughed. "Ha! Look at how your face is on fire! But you needn't be so embarrassed in front of me; I can tell you this sort of thing goes on in the Indian world just like here."

Mary's hands balled up into fists; she was at the end of her temper. She was about to lash out at him when she heard a voice say, "That'll be enough, laddie; you're insulting the girl."

She looked over to see McGregor standing by the corner of the cabin, an improvised crutch under his right shoulder. As she watched he dropped the crutch and walked with only the slightest limp until he was a foot away from Girty. Then he asked, "Might you tell me this fellow's name, Mary?"

"His name is Simon Girty, Tim. He's one of the hostages."

"Now, Simon, my good lad, I was listening from nearby. And I know you was just repeating a rumor you heard 'round the campfires. You bein' with the savages so long, I'm thinkin' you've just forgotten your manners when speakin' to a lass. But I'm sure you'll be wantin' to apologize to her for your thoughtlessness at speakin' such vile things."

Girty was a man of medium height and burly; but not as powerful as McGregor. He looked over the highlander and decided retreat was the better choice of the moment. He turned back to Mary and mumbled. "I, uh, am *indeed* sorry. I didn't mean to cause any discomfort, Miss. I just thought you would want to know what was bein' said around the camp."

McGregor clamped his hand on Girty's shoulder, none too gently. The young man winced.

"That was a fine apology lad. But now it's time for you to take yourself out of the girl's sight." He smiled at Girty, but there was no warmth in it. "And the thing is, I've been hearin' that they're sending some of the released hostages back to Pitt under escort tomorrow. I think you'll be wantin ' to make sure you're in that group, won't you, my fine lad?"

"Yes, yes I will. I am anxious to go back to the settlements."

"I thought you'd be seeing it that way, laddie. Now off you go."

McGregor and Mary watched until Girty disappeared around the corner of the cabin. Then McGregor winced and quickly moved over to lean against the side of the building. He sighed, "Mary, be a good girl and fetch me the crutch; I can't be standin' on my own much longer. And I need to get back to my blankets right away."

Mary brought him the crutch and then helped him get back to his tent. She said, "Tim, let me explain about what happened with Grenough. It's nothing like Girty was saying."

"Now Mary, there's no needin' of you to be sayin' anything. I don't believe a word that came out of his foul mouth. Besides, I know the whole true story."

In surprise, Mary asked, "How do you know what happened?"

Tim looked down at her and smiled broadly. "Now lass, Bob Kirkwood told me everything soon after it happened. And you know Kirkwood always knows the whole of what goes on or is being said in the regiment."

Mary gave him a quick kiss on the cheek. "Thanks for believing in me and protecting me, Tim."

Late that night, after she had gotten all the toddlers down to sleep, Mary sat on a log seat inside the nursery. Outside the rest of the staff was enjoying the campfire, talking and sharing laughter. But for once she didn't feel like joining them. It was the first time she had had some time to think things over since the encounter with Girty. She was dismayed to find that she was the subject of gossip and rumor throughout the camp about the affair with Grenough. Obviously her belief that the incident had been kept quiet had been a foolish illusion. And Laurie McPhie had clearly been repeating what she had seen to everyone who would listen. Undoubtedly she had embellished the story to make it more titillating to her listeners. She thought: *There are people in the regiment, probably a lot of them, who believe that I was literally in bed with Grenough. My God, they think I'm a harlot.*

A chill went through her body as she realized that the past few days had seen a complete reversal in her reputation. First she had lost the respect of the officers for violating regulations and essentially consorting with the enemy. And now there was apparently wide belief that she had had an affair with a man more than twice her age.

Mary had laid out her pallet in the nursery to keep watch on the children. She crawled into the blankets and settled down for the night. But sleep would not come and she spent hours tossing and turning. She finally dropped off to a slumber of exhaustion, but even then her brain would not leave her alone. A vivid dream came to her; she was in a room she could not leave and Grenough and Welford were together at a table, drinking from a tall bottle and laughing at her; laughing and making jokes about her plight and foolishness. Then she realized there were many tables of people all around her in the room and they had joined in the mirth at her expense. Then she saw Laurie McPhie sitting on top of one table, surrounded by a gaggle of men. Her legs dangled above the floor as she and all the men laughed together as they stared at Mary.

She felt rage growing in her and started yelling at them to shut their filthy mouths, but instead they just increased their laughing.

Finally, Mary woke up. She was startled to see a face, framed by blond hair, was above her barely visible in the dim moonlight which filtered into the cabin. Mary nearly screamed out thinking it was Laurie, but then she realized it was one of the toddlers, a little girl with blond tresses.

The girl said, "You were saying things and you scared me Miss Mary." Then she started crying and said, "I want my Mum and Da."

Mary got to her knees and hugged the little girl tightly. "It's all right; I want my Mum and Da too. I want them very much."

* * *

Early the next morning, with the frigid November dawn lighting up the sky, Joshua Baird appeared at the hospital just as Mary was finishing her breakfast. He was carrying his rifle and leading a saddled horse. Mary noticed that his saddle-bags, bedroll, and gray watchcoat were strapped to the saddle.

"I'm here to say goodbye, lass."

Mary asked, "Are you going out on a long scout?"

"No, Mary. The Indians have agreed to all Bouquet's demands. He's satisfied that the campaign is over. I'm going back as guide with the detachment which is escorting the hostages leaving today for Fort Pitt."

"Then I'll not see you until we get back to the fort."

125

"No, lass, I'll not be there. When we get to Pitt, I'm riding on to Carlisle with dispatches." He smiled. "Back there, I've got some convincin' to do with the Widow Downy. And if I'm successful, I'll be takin' her down to Winchester. The truth is, I don't know when I'll see you again."

Mary felt a fist grab her heart. *This was the last time she would ever see Joshua.* She reached out and wrapped her arms around him and put her head on his shoulder. She smelled his aroma; a combination of the man-smell from his clothing, the scent of his tobacco, and the faint whiff of whiskey on his breath. The fist holding her heart tightened, for it was the same smell she remembered when her father had hugged her just before marching off to his death on the great hill outside Fort Pitt. She took a deep breath, and then she suddenly thought of something she must say to Baird.

"Joshua, promise me something."

"Of course, Mary, what is it?"

"You must not tell Wend anything about what happened between Grenough and me."

"For God's sake! Why not lass?"

"It will just make him more determined to seek out Grenough for revenge. And that will put him in grave danger. The truth is, I hope he forgets about Grenough and stays home to raise his family."

"Yes, Mary, I see your point; I'll keep it to myself."

"And the same with the part about Abigail; don't let him know what happened between us. I don't want him knowing what I did or that we've even met. It will just keep his memory of me alive, and that might put me between him and his wife; I don't want there to be any chance of that happening."

Joshua sighed. "Mary, you are a fine girl with a great heart. Better than that scoundrel Wend deserves." He nodded and said, "Yes, I'll not say a word to Eckert."

At just that moment drums began beating the assembly down the line.

Joshua squeezed Mary and tenderly kissed her on the cheek. "I've got to be going now, lass. I know things will work out for you and you'll make me proud." Then he released her, turned, and quickly mounted the horse. As he did so, a groan escaped his lips. He looked down at Mary, shook his head, and said, "That damn leg again."

She looked up at him and put her hand on his leg. "Goodbye, Joshua, I'll always remember you."

The scout touched his heels to his mount and rode toward the sound of the drums. Then, after about twenty yards, he pulled up and spun the horse around.

resurrected from the grave. She stuttered as she tried to express her gratitude. "Sir, I am most grateful for the kindness of you and all these gentlemen."

"Not at all, Miss Fraser." Bouquet turned to Munro. "Surgeon, I have heard nothing except praise for Miss Fraser's service with the hospital. I personally witnessed her gallantry last year at Bushy Run. I'm sure you would appreciate the opportunity to add your letter to those from these other officers."

Munro looked flustered and appeared to be having trouble finding words. He looked at Mary and bit his lip, then he said, "Of course, of course, Colonel, it would indeed be my pleasure. Miss Fraser is a most competent nurse and an esteemed member of the hospital staff. I shall prepare a letter immediately."

Bouquet gathered up the papers in front of him and handed them to Welford. "Miss Fraser, the lieutenant will put all these letters in a dispatch case so that you can carry them with you in a way that will keep them from being lost or damaged."

Mary felt her eyes watering. She fought to hold back the tears, but despite her efforts, in a few seconds drops were streaming down her cheeks. Bouquet saw what was happening and came out from behind his desk. He produced a handkerchief and handed it to her.

"Miss Fraser, I believe that once before I told you that soldiers don't cry. You must learn to obey orders, or I shall find myself running out of handkerchiefs."

* * *

Just after dawn, MacDonald's convoy was forming up in the open area to the east of Fort Pitt. The three companies were mustering and the numerous wagons and carts were lined up in rows, their teams harnessed and ready, teamsters standing by with reins in hand. The wives and children of the soldiers were gathering in a tight group, ready to march at the rear of the column.

Mary stood near the base of the southeast bastion with Kirkwood and Tim McGregor. She was dressed in her marching outfit, her heavy pack lying on the ground beside her feet. The two men, as part of Stirling's company, would be wintering over in the fort. They had come to say goodbye to Mary and their other friends leaving in the convoy.

Kirkwood put his hand on McGregor's right shoulder. "Now Mary, take a look: There's something new the lad is wearing."

Mary looked at McGregor and suddenly realized he had a silver knot on his shoulder — the rank symbol of a corporal. "You've been promoted!"

A look of pride came over McGregor's face. "I just got it last night."

Kirkwood said, "Stirling promoted him to replace a corporal that was killed in the skirmish at the trader's camp. He said Tim deserved it, the way he was first in the charge and finished that warrior. And there ain't nobody in the company who don't agree, even if he is one of the newest men." Kirkwood again put his hand on McGregor's shoulder. "Stirling said he's a born soldier and has a bright future in the regiment."

Mary put her arm around McGregor's and said, "I'm very proud of you Tim. It's as rare honor to get a knot so soon."

The romantic ties between Mary and Tim had grown since his wounding in the skirmish. They had shared evenings beside the fire and many embraces, but Mary had not let it get any more intimate than that. Tim had not tried to push her further and Mary found that endearing about him. And now they would be separated for who knew how long. Rumor had it that the companies of the regiment would be scattered in garrison duties along Forbes Road and over the border country for an indefinite period.

Kirkwood looked over at the troop formation. "They'll be ready to go any time now, lass."

Mary said, "I'm going to miss you both. Perhaps your company will come east in the spring. After all, this is the second winter Stirling's men have had to spend here. If you come east, we'll be able be together then."

Kirkwood and McGregor looked at each other, then at Mary. Kirkwood said, "That's not in the cards, lass. We've just been told that when the weather breaks next spring, our company is going to be built up to a hundred men and Stirling is going to lead an expedition in boats down the Ohio and then up the Mississippi to relieve the French at Fort Chartres. We'll be there until the permanent British garrison from the 34th can come up the Mississippi from New Orleans. It could all take a year or more."

Kirkwood leaned over and gave Mary a brotherly kiss on her cheek. "I'll let you two alone to say goodbye." Then he walked off to speak with another group of men.

Mary said, "My God, Tim, it may be years till we see each other again."

McGregor looked at her with a twinkle in his eye. "Or perhaps never; think of what could happen on this trip."

"I know, but this is the army; we don't have control of where we go."

"It doesn't have be that way between us, Mary. You know I'm in love with you. And now that I'm a corporal, I'll be making more money. Marry me now and you can stay here this winter and go on the expedition with us."

Mary was only mildly surprised; she had guessed Tim had been working up to ask for her hand. She started to talk, but McGregor gently put his hand over her mouth to quiet her.

"Think on it Mary; think what an adventure we'd have on this trip; we'd be seeing wondrous places, magnificent birds, strange animals and new tribes of Indians. They say the Mississippi is a river near as wide as an ocean. And then there's New Orleans; we would rub shoulders with all the French and Spanish people, hear their strange lingo, taste their food. It's the chance of a lifetime, lass. And best of all we'd be together for the whole of it."

Finally, he took his hand back and then put his arms around her and kissed her passionately.

Mary returned his kiss, her body against his, and soon felt herself becoming aroused. It took all her mental strength to break it off.

"Tim, I'm tempted. And I can't deny I feel real affection for you."

"Then there's 'na reason to hesitate, lass. It's not too late for you to get your baggage from the wagon. And then we'll go see the chaplain in the fort."

"I'm sorry, Tim, I can't marry you."

He paused a moment, looking into her eyes. Then he said slowly, "You mean you *won't* marry me. And why, not lass?"

"For the same reason I told you at the beginning of the campaign. I've been preparing for life outside of the army since I was a small girl. And now, because of Bouquet and other officers, I have a real chance at that. But it's more than that. They've done much more for me than I could ever have expected. In a sense, if I don't follow through with what I've started, I'd be letting them down as much as myself."

The young man simply stared at her, apparently at a loss for words.

Mary reached out and put her hand on his arm. "Tim, believe this: I do truly love you. But the time is not right for me to marry. I must finish what I've started."

Mary's heart nearly broke when she saw the expression of grief on Tim's face when he realized the finality of her words. She searched for something to say to make him feel better.

But suddenly Ian Tavish, McDonald's personal piper, was there beside them. "Give him a last kiss Mary; it's time to go. McDonald's ready to march the column." Then he tapped McGregor on the shoulder and shook his hand. "If we don't see each other again in this world, lad, I vow we'll share a jug in hell." And then he was gone to round up other stragglers.

McGregor sighed, reached down and picked up Mary's pack. "Here, lass, turn around and I'll help you into the straps."

When they had finished, she turned to him, put her hand on his arm, and said, "Now listen to me, Tim, there's something you must promise me: When there's a fight or other trouble, stay close to Kirkwood. He's a rogue of the first order, but he'll always survive whatever happens. That's been proven many times and in many places. So stay with him, and listen to him, and I know you'll be all right."

McGregor laughed and nodded. "All right, lass. I'll promise you that."

Mary gave him a hug and a quick kiss. Then, without saying any more, she turned and walked off to join the other women.

As she walked, McGregor called out to her, "Mary Fraser, God go with you. And remember, it's not over between us!"

She looked back and grinned at him.

As she took her place among the women, Kathryn handed Mary the walking staff which she had been holding for her and said, "So, you're coming with us after all?"

"Yes, why wouldn't I?"

"Because everyone knew Timothy McGregor was going to ask you to marry him." Kathryn waved at their wagon. "I even made sure your bag was right by the tail gate so we could get it out easily."

Mary felt herself choke up. She closed her eyes and sighed. "Kathryn, there was a great fight between my heart and my head. In the end, my head won the battle. But I admit my heart is back there with Tim and I've never hurt like this before."

"You foolish girl; you can still grab your bag and run back to him."

"No, I'm going to do what I set out to do long ago. I've worked too hard to abandon it now."

"You know what I think? You've still got the love for that German fellow, Eckert, stuck in your heart, and its damn well keepin' you from thinkin' straight."

"For God's sake, Kathryn, he's married. I'll never see him again."

"Just the same, you won't let go of his memory. But lass, whatever's goin' through your mind, I'm telling you now, you're settin' yourself up to die a spinster."

Mary set her jaw. "There are worse things that could happen. I've made my choice and I'll live with it Kathryn."

Just then the drums sounded and under McDonald's orders, the companies swung into columns of fours and began marching for the beginning of Forbes Road. Soon the wagons had pulled out into line behind them, and finally it was the turn of the women and children to follow.

As they stepped off, Mary turned and looked back. McGregor and Kirkwood stood together at the base of the bastion. She gave them a final wave, as gaily as she could manage.

At the head of the column, the drums and pipes from all three companies had been massed together. The drummers were beating out a marching cadence. Presently the bagpipes joined in, their primal wailing raising the hair on the back of her neck as they always did.

As they advanced toward the tree line, Mary thought: I've marched to the sound of the drums and pipes for nine years. I've followed them to the wilds of Carolina, to the fever-ridden West Indies, across the rivers of Ohio, and over Forbes Road more times than I can remember. They've led me to love and to battle, to the death of my parents, and to a wound which nearly killed me. But now, for the first time, the drums are leading me in pursuit of my own destiny and the life I've set for myself.

Mary reached down and touched the leather dispatch case which hung at her side and thought of the letters inside. The knowledge that they were there gave her a feeling of hope and strength.

And suddenly she was surprised to realize that at the very same time there was a great ache in her heart about leaving Tim McGregor, her spirits were soaring. Around her, other women and children were turning for a last look at the hulking fortress behind them. But Mary Fraser marched with her eyes straight to the front, steeling herself to think only of the new life which lay ahead.

AUTHOR'S NOTES

AND ACKNOWLEDGEMENTS

This third book in the Forbes Road Series was written to tell the story of the final military operation of Pontiac's Uprising — the 1764 march of a combined British and provincial expedition into the Ohio Country. The intent was to force the warring tribes to enter into peace negotiations and submit to British rule. The campaign was successful, but tragically, the expedition also proved to be the last significant achievement of Henry Bouquet's life. He died of yellow fever at Pensacola, Florida in 1765 just as he was about to take up command of British forces in the southern colonies. Although the campaign is considered a model of frontier military planning and logistics, achieving its major goals with virtually no combat, its very success has led to it often being treated as a footnote to history. I hope that readers of *The Camp Follower Affair* will have gained some appreciation of the challenges which faced Bouquet and the men and women of his small command.

The following are some random notes regarding the history of the expedition, my speculation about various aspects of the campaign, and as usual, confessions of my most grievous sins committed in the interest of creating an entertaining story about one of the crucial but little known events in America's colonial history.

Mary Fraser as Protagonist. Since publication of *Forbes Road* and *Conestoga Winter,* many readers have inquired about the future of Mary Fraser in the series, the general sentiment being hope that her role would not end with *Conestoga Winter.* Author's disclosure: It was always the intent to have her return at some point, either in the Forbes Road Series or later in the upcoming Revolutionary Series. So when the concept of a novella to complete the story of Pontiac's Rebellion and to fill the gap between *Conestoga Winter* and the final book of the Forbes Road Series, *Lord Dunmore's Folly,* matured in my mind, Mary was the logical protagonist. She was well positioned as a nurse with the 42nd Foot to witness the major events of the 1764 campaign. Wend was not available because, pursuant to the series storyline, he had become in large degree persona non grata in Pennsylvania as a result of his actions in *Conestoga Winter*. In any case he was busy establishing his family and business in Winchester, Virginia during the period of this story.

Black Powder to the Ohio Tribes. While the pack train of Grenough's war supplies that Mary and Joshua discover in Chapter Six is of course fictional, it is a matter of record that the tribes were receiving ammunition from outside sources. For example, in *Never Come to Peace Again*, the late David Dixon points out that the Shawnee received 1,600 pounds powder in a pack train from French traders during the period that Bouquet's force was on the Muskingum. Like some Indians, there were still French traders and hunters who naively believed that a successful tribal rebellion had the potential to bring the French government back into the picture. But by 1764, this was truly a fantasy.

The Question of Combat. Most historical narratives of the campaign describe it as a relentless, essentially bloodless advance through the Ohio Country which eventually forced the tribal chiefs to come to negotiations. I am not aware of any substantial discussion of casualties in contemporary academic literature. Moreover, the only indication of combat casualties in either the Bouquet Papers or Bouquet's Orderly Book is the death of a light horseman in the field who is assumed to have been killed by hostiles. However, in researching this book, I came across an old manuscript on the website *Electric Scotland* entitled, *Military Annals of the Highland Regiments*. In the section which describes the Black Watch's participation in the 1764 Ohio expedition, it states that there were significant skirmishes with the tribal warriors as the force advanced. The manuscript also shows a table of Black Watch casualties during the regiment's campaigns in colonial America during the French and Indian War era. The line referring to Bouquet's expedition of 1764 reports seven killed in action and ten wounded. The casualties cited in this table for other campaigns are consistent with those reported in more recent published works. Thus, at a minimum, it can be said that there is evidence of some level of combat resulting in casualties during the march to the Muskingum. This evidence was sufficient for me to unsheathe my author's creative license and, for dramatic purposes, conflate the occurrence of minor combat with the supplying of war supplies to the Indians to produce the fictional skirmish presented in Chapter Seven.

Timing of the Expedition. As highlighted in the narrative, the expedition was up against the onset of winter weather, a factor which put severe constraints on Bouquet's operational flexibility. Eighteenth century armies were generally not equipped to campaign in winter months and usually went into winter camp in a place where good shelter and provisions could be found. This often entailed dispersing the force into detached garrisons to ease the gathering of provisions for men and forage for animals. In this case, the occurrence of sustained winter storms including snow and icing could have proved disastrous for a force operating more than 100 wilderness miles —and across a major river — from its nearest base. Moreover, Bouquet could carry only limited provisions with the force and effective resupply would have been almost impossible.

As background, Bouquet had originally planned to advance into the Ohio Country in 1763, immediately after relieving Fort Pitt. However, following the battle of Bushy Run in August, it became clear that the pick-up field force of regulars at his disposal (Around 400 effectives after the battle) was insufficient for the planned campaign. Moreover, the detachment of the 77th Highlanders which made up nearly a quarter of that force was overdue to be sent back to Scotland for disbandment. In any case, logistic support available at the time was totally inadequate for an advance beyond Fort Pitt. Therefore, the start of the expedition was necessarily delayed until late spring/early summer 1764. However, even this goal proved unattainable, primarily due to foot dragging of the colonial governments in recruiting men, authorizing funding, and obtaining sufficient supplies and transport. In these matters Pennsylvania was particularly reticent. However, the January-February Paxton Boy Insurrection showed that the pacifist element in Philadelphia could no longer ignore the demands of the border settlers for assistance in their defense. This, and arm twisting by British authorities, led to legislation to re-raise the Pennsylvania Regiment and contribute to necessary funding and logistic support. Virginia and Maryland more readily provided volunteers and support.

Bouquet used Carlisle and Fort Loudoun as staging bases to marshal his forces and then sent off convoys of troops and supplies along Forbes Road to Fort Pitt, wherein the final assembly and organization of the expedition took place. Bouquet himself arrived at Pitt on September 18th. The force was in place and ready to advance on October 1, but this essentially left a maximum of eight weeks for reasonably safe campaigning and the conclusion of peace negotiations before the weather could be expected to close in. Under the circumstances he was facing,

Bouquet did a masterful job in putting together the expedition and getting it underway even by October. In summary, it can be said that this eighteenth century soldier fully understood the modern war college saying that "Amateurs talk tactics, professionals talk logistics."

British Order of Battle. Numerically, Bouquet's force for the 1764 expedition was the equivalent of a small brigade, consisting of a mix of regular troops, provincials, and militia. (See discussion of "Military Forces in Colonial America" in Author's Notes section of *Conestoga Winter*). Effective combatant strength was about 1200 men. Bouquet had originally postulated a force of 1800-2000, but soon found that number unattainable. The units and their approximate strength were:

1st Battalion 60th Foot, Royal Americans (3 companies present – 113 men under direct command of Major Mark Prevost)

1st Battalion 42nd Foot, Royal Highland Regiment (6 companies present – 316 men under Lieutenant Colonel John Field)

1st Battalion Pennsylvania Regiment (Provincials, 4 companies- 233 men under Lieutenant Colonel Turbutt Francis)

2nd Battalion Pennsylvania Regiment (Provincials, 4 companies- 218 men, under Lieutenant Colonel Asher Clayton)

Field's Corps of Virginia Volunteers (Militia rifleman/rangers, 82 men, under Major John Field)

McNeill's Corps of Virginia Volunteers (Militia riflemen/rangers, 138 men, under Lieutenant Colonel John McNeill)

Maryland Volunteers (1 militia company of about 43 men, under Captain William McClellan joined at Fort Pitt, a second of similar size under Captain John Wolgomatt joined at the Muskingum)

Light Horse Squadron (Piper's and Kerns' Troops, estimated about 40 men each troop; these were part of the Pennsylvania Regiment, Piper's troop associated with the 2nd Battalion, Kerns' with the 1st and their numbers are contained in the strength of the appropriate battalion above.)

Miscellaneous scouts, volunteers, allied Indian warriors amounting to about 50 individuals.

(Note: This list was compiled from discussions of the expedition organization in McCulloch's *Sons of the Mountains, Volume 1*, Matt Wulff's *Henry Bouquet's Destiny*, and *Bouquet's Orderly Book, Volume 1* with explanations/footnotes by Edward G. Williams)

Of note is the low effective strength of the Pennsylvania battalions. They had originally been authorized to have an establishment of roughly 500 each; in fact when assembled at the beginning of the campaign at Carlisle, together the two units mustered a total of around 950. Their numbers were soon reduced by a high desertion rate (reports indicate 200 disappeared by the time the column arrived at Fort Loudoun) and the detachment of units to form the garrisons of forts along Forbes Road. In addition, because of the haste in which these two units had been raised, their initial military skills and discipline were hardly more than that of militia.

Bouquet also had some problems with his regulars. The British infantry was undergoing the process of reorganization to the post -Seven Years war peacetime establishment. Battalion authorized strength was being reduced from about 1000 to around 500. Despite the value shown by light infantry in the French war and Pontiac's Rebellion, the new battalion organization went from ten companies to nine by elimination of the light infantry company. Regardless of the impending change, Bouquet kept light infantry companies of the two regular regiments active for the campaign. In addition, the second battalion of the Black Watch had been disbanded as had the third and fourth battalions of the Royal Americans. This led to considerable personnel turbulence, particularly in the commissioned ranks as numerous officers changed assignments (as driven by the dictates of seniority) or left the service. As noted in the narrative, men from the 77th Foot and the 2nd Battalion of the Black Watch were drafted into the remaining battalion of the 42nd to fill out company strength. The 1st Battalion Royal Americans was seriously understrength because of the massacres of outpost fort garrisons at the onset of Pontiac's Uprising, expiration of enlistments, and desertion. Thus even the regulars weren't as "shaken down" as might have been expected. Bouquet did conduct significant training at Loudoun and Pitt before the advance began and, of course, he did drill the entire force in his special formations for marching, defense, and fortified encampments. It is a testament to Bouquet's professionalism that he was able to forge a cohesive, tactically proficient force out of these disparate units.

Light Horse Troops. The two light horse troops mentioned in the narrative played an important role in the campaign. They are not to be confused with standard European light dragoon formations of the period but were instead Bouquet's own innovation for forest warfare. They were essentially mounted infantry, having sufficient mobility to conduct far-ranging patrols but who would mostly fight on foot. Bouquet specified their basic arms to be a rifle (preferably a short barreled rifle like the Jaeger model which German gunsmiths had brought over from the old country) and a long-handled axe. Certainly they also carried knives and in some cases, personally owned pistols. They became the utility troops of the campaign, patrolling, dispatch riding, forming part of the advance or the rearguard of the formation, at times helping to clear the way for the column with their axes. Because of the shortage of pack animals, about half of each troop's mounts were initially used as pack-horses to carry provisions for the first few days after leaving Pitt; these supplies were consumed first and then the light horsemen were available for their primary mission.

Engineer Thomas Hutchins. Hutchins, a native of New Jersey, is one of the underappreciated figures of the American colonial and early republic period. As discussed in the narrative, he laid out Fort Pitt at the Forks of the Ohio in 1758-59. Later he worked as an Indian agent within Sir William Johnson's organization and traveled the Great Lakes territory and Ohio Country in the early 1760's. He was originally assigned to be the assistant engineer of the 1764 expedition, but assumed full responsibility when the primary engineer had to drop out due to illness. While at Fort Pitt, Bouquet tasked him to plan the route of the campaign, based on his knowledge of the Ohio Country, a job which he accomplished with great skill. Once the operation was underway, the maps he produced of the actual route through the wilderness were extremely accurate given his rudimentary instruments and stand up well today in comparison to those produced with modern technology. At Bouquet's direction, he also made a map showing the layout and topography of the Bushy Run Battlefield which is reproduced in virtually every reference on the battle.

After the outbreak of the revolution, now with the rank of captain, Hutchins remained in the British Army on engineering/surveying duties in Florida until 1777, a service which did not put him in direct conflict with rebel forces. After that he sailed to England to get a book published. However, his colonial roots put him under suspicion and he was imprisoned when found to have correspondence from friends who were known rebels in his possession. He later cleared himself of any disloyal actions, sold his commission in the Army, and traveled to France where he gained the attention and support of Benjamin Franklin. He returned to America in time to become Engineer of Nathaniel Greene's Southern Army in 1781.

Subsequently, in recognition of his service and abilities, Congress accorded Hutchins the title of Geographer of the United States. In this role he set about producing maps of the new country and he established a coordinate survey system which divided the land into sections, townships, and ranges. This system is the basis of the Public Land Survey System of today. He also was the advocate of an expedition to explore the western part of the continent, from the Mississippi to the Pacific coast; some of the planning he did in preparation for such a journey was helpful to Lewis and Clark nearly twenty years later. Hutchins died in 1787 at Pittsburgh.

Charlot Kaske. This individual of mixed ancestry was indeed one of the most vocal and influential Shawnee proponents of continuing the rebellion against the British. He had attracted a significant numbers of aggressive young warriors to his cause. However, in a major error of timing, he had actually left the Ohio Country just before the arrival of Bouquet's force. As Joshua Baird pointed out to Mary in the narrative, he was journeying westward to Fort Chartres to appeal for assistance from the French. Failing in that objective, he traveled down the Mississippi to New Orleans to seek assistance directly from the French Governor of Louisiana. Thus the reader will realize that, for dramatic purposes and to illustrate the conflict within Shawnee tribal leadership, I have somewhat changed the timeline by including him as an active leader in the fictional events surrounding the destruction of Grenough's pack train by Piper and Stirling. However, it is interesting to note that Charlot Kaske subsequently returned to the Illinois/Ohio area in time to cross paths with Stirling's spring 1765 expedition to relieve the French garrison at Chartres. After a short confrontation, Kaske realized the futility of further resistance and negotiated a truce with Stirling.

References for Further Reading. In recent years, *a* multitude of books have been published on the French & Indian War, Pontiac's Uprising, and the British and colonial military during that period. Digitalized versions of older books are now available on the internet. I found the following useful in researching Bouquet's expedition and concocting Mary Fraser's fictional role in the campaign:

The Orderly Book of Colonel Henry Bouquet's Expedition Against the Ohio Indians, 1764 (Orderly Book #1, Carlisle to Fort Pitt) (Privately printed after 1960, Digitalized and available on line) Edited by Edward G. Williams

The Orderly Book of Colonel Henry Bouquet's Expedition Against the Ohio Indians, 1764 (Orderly Book #2, The march to the Muskingum) (1960, Privately Printed, Digitalized and available on line). Edited by Edward G. Williams

The Papers of Henry Bouquet, Volume VI, November 1761 to July 1765 (Pennsylvania Historical and Museum Commission, 1994 Edition)

Never Come to Peace Again: Pontiac's Uprising and the Fate of the British Empire in North America, (University of Oklahoma Press, 2005) David Dixon

Henry Bouquet's Destiny: The March to Bushy Run. (Independently Published, 2014) Matt Wulff

Sons of the Mountains: The Highland Regiments in the French & Indian War, Volumes I and II, (Purple Mountain Press, 2006) Ian Macpherson McCulloch

Redcoats: The British Soldier and War in the Americas, 1755-1763 (Cambridge University Press, 2002) Stephen Brumwell

The Shawnees and the War For America, (Viking Penguin, 2007) Colin G. Colloway

The Middle Ground: Indians, Empires, and Republics in the Great Lakes Region, 1650-1815 (Cambridge University Press, 1991) Richard White. Note: Contains a good summary of Charlot Kaske's role in Pontiac's Uprising and the aftermath.

Defenders of the Frontier: Colonel Henry Bouquet and the Officers and Men of the Royal American Regiment, 1763-1764 (Heritage Books, 2007) Kenneth P. Stuart

Through So Many Dangers: The Memoirs and Adventures of Robert Kirk, Late of the Royal Highland Regiment, (Purple Mountain Press, 2004) Robert Kirk (Or Kirkwood), Edited by Ian McCulloch and Timothy Todish. Note: This is a modern presentation of the book published in 1775 by the man called Corporal Robert Kirkwood in this novella and the novel *Forbes Road*.

Acknowledgements. I am indebted to many people for their assistance in preparation of this third volume of the Forbes Road Series. Pamela Patrick White extended permission for the use of her painting, *The Camp Followers*, for the cover and for promotional purposes. Her portfolio of historical artwork can be viewed online at www.whitehistoricalart.com. David Miller, the former Site Educator (Historian) at Bushy Run Battlefield, read the draft manuscript, provided numerous insights on the 1764 campaign, and clarified details of Bouquet's march route through Ohio. Major John Chapman, USMC (Ret) did his usual fine job of reading and critiquing the draft. I'm extremely grateful to my wife, Cathy, who provided continuous encouragement and content review of the manuscript, supplying a much necessary female perspective on a story about a young woman. Mostly I'm grateful for her patience with my reclusive ways while I was immersed in historical tomes or hovering for long hours over the keyboard. And, as always, I'm personally buoyed by the interest shown by readers of the series who have contacted us through the website or the postal service.

Robert J Shade
February 2015

Made in the USA
Middletown, DE
25 November 2015